Destroying GAGE

Bloody Saints MC Book 2

Roxanne Greening

Dedicated to my husband and kids for their love and support. To my dad and my mom for making me who I am today. And the rest of my family for all their support!

Text Copyright 2019 © Roxanne Greening

All Rights Reserved

All rights reserved in all media. No part of this book may be used or reproduced without written permission. Except in the case of brief quotations embodied in critical articles and reviews.

The moral rights of Destroying Gage as the author of this work has been asserted by her in accordance with the copyright, designs, and patients act of 1988.

This is a work of fiction. All names, characters, locales, and incidents are the products of the author's imagination and any resemblance to places or events is coincidental or fictionalized.

Published in the United States of America 2019

Trademark Acknowledge

The author and publisher Acknowledge the trademark status and trademark ownership of all the trademarks, service marks and word marks mentioned in this book.

About The Author:

Roxanne Greening is a mother of two young children and lives in the beautiful rural area in West Virginia, USA. It was because of her love for reading romances, that Roxanne decided to write her own. However, it is the MC romances that she enjoys writing the most. "Being able to become a rebel, an outlaw (in fiction) is a powerful thing." And so, Axel, the first book of the SONS OF THE APOCALYPSE, was published in August 2016.

Her comedy nonfiction, The Rantings of a Crazy Person, was born out of demands from her family and friends to write about her own experiences. And her children's book, The chronicles of rocky and binx aka the steam punk kid and the angel of death. Titanic's Doom! Came from wanting to write a book for her son who suffers from ADHD.

Roxanne also enjoys to quilt, and secretly wants to be a ninja.

Follow Me

Facebook- http://ow.ly/mMVp30jtWMx
Twitter- Twitter.com/@RoxanneGreening
My Amazon page- http://ow.ly/a9o930jtX6n
Www.authorroxannegreening.wordpress.com
Goodreads- http://ow.ly/vR9K30cBq8R
Instagram.com/authorroxannegreening
BookBub- http://ow.ly/JXVH30jtWFx

Other Ways To Contact Me:

Authorroxannegreening@yahoo.com

Author Roxanne Greening

P.O. Box 624

Parkersburg, W.V. 26101

Prologue:

Two Years Ago.

What I just saw would live in my dreams for the rest of my life. He was a monster, and there was no way I was marrying the likes of him.

He just killed her. His wife. I knew we were supposed to marry, and I had been confused about this. It was some sick joke. Zec was devastatingly good looking. Any of us ladies would be lucky to have him as our husband.

That is if he wasn't already married. My father had informed me a month ago that Zec was going to be my husband.

I knew better than to voice my confusion. Zec had been married for the last four years. As the boss, he needed an heir, and it was something that he still didn't have.

At thirty, he was our youngest boss. He killed his father for the position two years ago. His younger brother Besin was now the second in command.

Besin had this fallen angel look to him just as his older brother, but the cold calculation wasn't as noticeable. Both of them terrified me.

Besin had been watching Savanna for weeks now, and I knew deep down he would ask for her hand. My friend was going to find herself in a dark, scary marriage just like I would. A fate we wouldn't survive intact.

Zec's hand had been wrapped around her throat. His wife's eyes had this dull appearance to them. She had been expecting this, and I think there was a flash of relief as he put the gun to her head and pulled the trigger.

My heart stopped beating. The air literally turned to dust in my lungs. Zec and Besin were here at my father's for an extended visit. Both were staying the night, and now I knew why.

"It's a shame you had to kill her," Besin said coldly.

"She wouldn't bear me a son," Zec replies with a careless shrug.

A fucking shrug like he didn't just shoot his wife. Like he didn't just take an innocent life. Bile rose up my throat. It burned, and I almost choked as I fought to swallow it back down.

"Roslin will give me beautiful children," Zec tells Basin.

"Perfect children just like Savanna will give me," Basin tells Zec with a smile.

My heartbeat started beating faster. I had seen what they did to his wife before Zec killed her. Besin had called it an honor, and I called it a horror.

"Will you share Roslin if she gets pregnant?" Besin asked.

Shudders raked my body so hard, I had to fight to stay standing.

"No, she will be all mine," Zec growls.

Should I be relieved he wasn't going to allow his brother to touch me? More bile. Her screams still echoed in my ears. Tears streaked my cheeks over and over.

I couldn't marry him. I wouldn't marry him. I waited for what felt like hours as they discussed different things. I was stuck in my hiding spot as her body cooled. I stared lifelessly between the wall and her crumpled body on the floor.

They just left her there like discarded trash. Now that they've had their fun, she was no longer useful. I never spoke to her, but I knew no one deserved what happened to her, and no one should be left to rot on the floor.

Chapter 1

Ronnie

Three Years Ago.

I had seen my father open that safe many times. Not once was he concerned about me watching. We were more like furniture to him. Raised to be pretty little statues.

The door opened silently, and I thanked my lucky stars. My father hated when it creaked, so he kept the hinges nice and oiled.

This was the night that I planned on leaving. I grabbed two more stacks of cash and sighed. The oversized purse that I bought two months ago was going to be overflowing with money. Heavy couldn't even begin to describe it.

In total, I was sure that I had stolen over a hundred thousand dollars. No one noticed, and I thought it was beyond a miracle.

I had only one thing left to do before I disappeared. Call Savanna. I pulled out my phone to say goodbye to the one person whom I loved more than anything. The one person that I had seen as my little sister. Savanna was only a year younger than me, making her nineteen. Only one more year before they would be marrying her off.

The call was hard to make. The sound of Savanna's voice made it difficult to tell her about Besin. If I made it, maybe she could as well. Dropping the phone into the trash, I turned away from the only life I've ever known.

The night swallowed me as I ran for my life, for my future. Even if I only made it a day, it would be worth the risk. My biggest fear was that Zec would still want me if they caught me.

Chapter 2

Ronnie

Two Years and Nine Months Ago.

I had been running for weeks. Never staying in one place more than a day or two. I have yet to see any signs of my father or Zec.

I bought a blond wig and changed my clothes. Shopping at a supercenter was way different than the boutiques that I normally shopped in. It was fun, and I cherished that no one knew me. I was just like everyone else.

The jeans that I bought made me feel like a rebel. I pulled my long brown hair into a ponytail, deciding on not using the wig. In this town, I was going to go natural. The big sunglasses will help, so no need for the fake hair.

Looking in the mirror, I felt more like myself than I ever have. My long brown locks no longer reached my hips. I had cut about fifteen inches off, taking it to just above the middle of my back.

My hotel room was clean, but it wasn't the five star I normally would have stayed in had I been with my family. Not that we stayed in many hotels. In fact, before I left, I had only stayed one night in a hotel.

Smiling, I slipped the big sunglasses on. My biggest purchase so far was my car. It was a used car, but it was also a beast on wheels.

It cost me five grand for this beautiful black Tahoe. It blended and gave me more options. I climbed into the beast and settled in my seat before buckling up and turning the key. The loud rumble caused another smile to stretch over my face.

Freedom was a beautiful thing.

Chapter 3

Gage

Two Years Ago.

The cell was so small. I fucking hated this place. I had a little less than a year left. Seven months and I would be out of this hell hole.

The bars all around seem to be mocking me. My only view this past year has been the cold, stone walls and the metal bars in front of me.

I got told what type of food to eat and when to eat it. I was also told when I could go outside. This place killed souls. I watched men come in here thinking they were king shit only to be taken down more than a few pegs.

We lived in housing units. It was a group of cells put together where we could mingle during the day. I watched as one of the guys tattooed one of the younger inmates.

Sticks was a badass with an ink gun. His work was beautiful. The fucker he was tattooing was green as fuck. He came in here and has yet to figure out how to keep his damn shoes.

Sticks was only charging him for a few snacks. It caused some of the others to back off. It seems Sticks liked him. Good, maybe the kid would survive. Hopefully, Sticks didn't get moved before Greenie learned how to live in these walls.

Today was visitation day. The brothers planned to come see me, but I turned them down. Fucking Crow wouldn't take no for an answer though.

Rodney approached with a smile. I liked Rodney. He was one of the favored guards around here. He was not one to look down on someone. He treated us like humans and had earned a lot of respect. Anyone that fucked with Rodney found themselves in medical.

"Looking good, Sticks," Rodney called out.

Sticks didn't pause. He just shouted out, "Thanks, man."

Tattooing here wasn't exactly allowed. Rodney looked the other way. He gave us more freedom than was allowed. We weren't caged animals in his eyes, just misplaced people. His words, not ours.

"Come on, Gage," Rodney tells me.

"Dammit, Crow," I sighed.

"You know he isn't going to listen to you, Gage. It's good to get a glimpse of the outside world. A reminder of where home is," Rodney patted me on the back before cuffing me. It was routine, and I knew he didn't like it any more than we did.

The visitation room was open. Just a few octagon picnic tables which were all metal and welded to the concrete floor. They were painted gray and peeling and in need of a fresh coat. My thumb went to one of the flakes of paint and flicked it off.

"What the fuck, Crow," I snapped.

"Don't take that fucking tone with me," he snarled back.

"I didn't want any visitors," I told him darkly.

"You now have money in your account. Go buy some shit and be happy," Crow sighed.

I just stared at him. I appreciated the money, but I fucking hated the visits. It reminded me that I was locked away in a cage and not out riding my bike and enjoying the open road.

"How're things out there?" I couldn't help but ask.

"Fucking boring without you," Crow quips.

I laughed. The fucker.

"New ink?" He asked, pointing to the tattoo on my arm.

"Yeah, Sticks is fucking amazing," I tell him with a shrug.

"When he gets out, tell him to come to the club," Crow tells me.

"Sticks isn't getting out. He's a lifer," I tell Crow quietly.

Sticks was never seeing the outside. It was something that he didn't give two shits about. Guess being a killer for a mob leached your damn feelings.

"Anything we can do for him?" Crow asked.

Sticks had it good. The family he was from kept his accounts full and the guards in his housing unit well paid. He gave the ultimate sacrifice, and they kept him happy.

"Nah, he's good," I tell him with a nod of thanks.

Sticks was my friend and the only motherfucker in this place I cared about. He said us killers needed to stick together. But it was more than that. There were a shit ton of killers here, but only a few were in his good graces.

Sticks ran our housing unit, and I was like his second. His words, not mine. I wanted to keep my head down and my nose clean. Sticks was a cold, calculating, scary motherfucker. What he said goes. Period. Or he'd kill you and laugh while doing it.

I've seen him do it more than once, and the government just keeps him here in this prison, which was a lower security prison. How the fuck that worked was beyond me.

"The club isn't the same without you," Crow tells me.

"You growing a vagina?" I ask him. Shit, he sounded like a woman.

"Fuck you, asshole. My dick is just fine," he snarled.

"So, you say," I give him a shrug.

"I'll fucking show you," he snapped while standing up.

"Keep it in your pants, I don't want to see your dick. I'm pretty sure it would result in you wearing a matching jumpsuit," I tell him with a laugh.

"Found an old lady," Crow tells me with a smile.

Something in me clenched. There was a small yearning for just what Crow was talking about. I wanted to smack myself. I didn't need my dick tied down, but I missed women. That's it.

"Lucky fucker," I tell him with a glare. Shit, there were a few pussies available in here, but none that I would touch. There were two female guards and a doctor.

I know a few of the guys pounded them, but I kept my dick clear of anyone who told me what to do, period. Those bitches held the rains, and I wanted nothing to do with that.

"Fuck, man. I'm sorry," Crow sighed.

"Don't worry about it, man. I'm happy for your ass," I tell him. It's the truth. He needed a woman to settle him.

"We'll have a big ass party when you finally get out of this shit hole," he smiled.

I've seen worse prison's than this, and I shrug. That shit was months away.

"A lot of shits gone down since you've been gone. Church the morning after the party," Crow gives my shoulder a squeeze. Rodney watches but does nothing.

I see some of the other guards approaching a few of the inmates. Times up.

"Stop coming here," I tell Crow as I stand up.

"Don't fucking tell me what to do, Gage. I'll be here next week," he snaps at me.

"It's not fucking safe for you, prez," I sigh.

"Let me worry about my ass, and you worry about yours," he laughed as he walked away. The dick.

"Come on inmate 195178," Rodney tells me. That's what you were in here. A fucking number.

I knew he hated using our numbers, but sometimes he had too, and now was one of those times. Nodding, I stood up and walked in front of Rodney. Never behind.

They knew better than to give us their backs. Seven more months. Then I was free of this boring as fuck existence. That's exactly what you did here, exist.

Chapter 4

Ronnie

Two Years Ago.

I had bought this house a week ago. It was time to find some roots, as I was tired as fuck of running. I haven't seen any of them. Not one.

Maybe they've given up? I snort, yeah, right. There have been so many times that I've wanted to go pick up some guy and take him to my bed or even his, but I couldn't do it.

Disgust filled me again as I walked around the corner. Was I truly free if I couldn't do the one thing that would set me completely free?

Because it wouldn't. I knew this. I've always known this. My eyes darted around as I scanned my surroundings, a habit that I hope I'd never give up. It was survival, never get too comfortable.

My foot hit something, and it sent me to my knees. Pain flew up my arms and down to my knees. Then, a small groan reached my ears, and it didn't come from me.

Sitting back, I turned my head to look at what I tripped over. Something caused my bags to fly out of my hands, and I saw the blood that covered my knees.

The girl was covered with bruises, and she was coated with blood. Her naked body was exposed to the world, and my eyes stung as I took in her helpless position. Who the fuck did this? Then, the blond hair had me sucking in a deep breath.

Savanna? Oh, god, my heart exploded from my chest. My eyes once again looked around the empty alley. No one was in sight. Could they be hiding?

She was still a year away from getting married. They wouldn't have given her to him yet, or would they? Tears spilled over my cheeks as my chest heaved. I did this to her, to my friend, to my sister.

With a shaking hand, I grabbed her shoulder and turned her to me. Relief washed over me only to be filled with shame. It wasn't Savanna, but it was still a woman who went through, who the fuck knows what kind of hell.

"Help me," she croaked.

Her eyes were fused closed as they were so swollen. My chest constricted. I couldn't leave her here.

"Save my baby," she whispered painfully.

My eyes darted to her stomach. There was a very slight roundness to it. If she hadn't told me, I would never have known. It was literally the only unmarred spot on her body.

"I've got you," I tell her as I look for some way to get her to my car. It was only a few feet away, but could I carry her? I wasn't so sure. I might have to drag her.

My eyes went to the trunk of my car. I had a go bag in there. An "oh, shit, I need to get the fuck out now" bag.

She needed clothes, something to cover her and give her some damn dignity.

"I'll be right back," I tell her gently.

"Please, don't leave me," she cried weakly.

"I'm not leaving you here, I promise," I tell her as I climb to my feet. Rushing to the car, I popped the truck listening as the latch released.

I quickly unzipping the bag, and I all but ripped it open as I dove inside of it. I had a pair of soft flannel pajama bottoms and a matching soft t-shirt. Pulling them out, I closed the truck quietly.

Scanning the alley again, I made sure we haven't drawn attention. I ran back to the girl and lifted her up by her shoulders.

"I'm going to put these clothes on you. I need a little help, though, can you do it?" I asked, keeping my tone light. As if seeing her damn near death was nothing. I didn't want to terrify her any more than she was.

Pushing the sleeves up her arms, I tugged the top over her head and gently lifted it over her exposed breasts. My eyes once again darted to her slight bump.

"Good," I praised her. "Let's get these pants on. You'll feel so much better."

I knew that I would if I was her out her naked. Although, what the fuck did I know. Maybe nakedness was the last thing from her mind.

I lifted one leg then her other. I put her feet through the leg holes then pulled the material slowly up her legs. There were cuts and bruises all over her white skin.

More tears filled my eyes. My heart was literally bleeding for her, and the memories of why I left were knocking, begging to be free.

His wife looked like this when they… no stop. This woman needs me, I can't go back there.

She lifted her hips, and I gave a quick tug and sighed when she was covered. I then slipped one arm under her legs and the other behind her back. I winced as she hissed.

I tried to lift her. I gave it my all, even grunting with the effort. But let's face it, I wasn't raised to be strong, and I never found the time or felt safe enough to go to the gym.

"I'm sorry. I'm going to have to drag you to my car," I tell her, my voice was fighting the tears that wanted to escape. I didn't want her to know that I was crying. She needed me to be strong for her.

"It's okay," she whispered.

It wasn't, and we both knew it. I grabbed her arms and looked behind me. Thank fuck for the grass! We would only be on the black tar for maybe a foot before we reached my car.

I started to tug and gave it my all. I wasn't leaving her behind. 'Save her' was currently chanted over and over in my head. Once we reached the tar, I cringed. This was going to hurt.

"I'm going to let go so I can open the car door," I paused and swallowed before I told her about the pain to come. "There's about a foot of pavement between you and my car."

She nodded gently. We both knew what was coming, and she accepted it. I promised myself this was the last time someone would hurt her. I would do what I couldn't do and what I haven't done for Savanna. I was going to protect and save her from whatever and whoever did this.

For the first time, the gun resting in the holster at my back had a better purpose. I was going to save us both.

Chapter 5

Ronnie

Two Years Ago.

I dreamed of a future with freedom from the forced, elegant life that I had. Not once in my short time of freedom did I feel as free as I did at this moment.

The fact that it was because of this poor battered woman made me feel like shit. She deserved more than my misplaced gratitude.

Her whimpers made my eyes tear up. I had no idea what she had been through, not really. My imagination had gone wild with all the possibilities.

Her jaw was so swollen she couldn't talk, and her eyes were still swollen, but she could at least see through small slits.

She's vomited and barely kept any of the liquid protein shakes that I was trying to force down her throat. I cringed at the memory of how I had to drag her into the house.

The blanket that I collected from inside helped to protect her abused flesh. I hated every moment, and every pull on that blanket.

I was thankful for the privacy that I had gotten by living in this tiny town. My house was shaded by trees, and my driveway was longer than any of the others.

This house was a shit hole when I bought it a few months ago. I sanded the floors, painted the walls, and used cheap stick down tiles in the kitchen and the bathroom.

I was constantly watching DIY shows, trying to learn how to do all of this. Each update, each drop of sweat, every tear of discomfort was worth it. I've never in my old life done any of this.

I would have been a breeder, a fucking broodmare, and nothing more. Just arm candy that kept her mouth shut and probably would have been a shell of myself. Lost in the sea of pain. Sometimes I wondered how long it would have taken for him to break me.

The thought of Savanna's beautiful face framed by her long straight hair made my heart clench. My eyes went back to the broken girl on the couch, which was the furthest she made it in the house. I hope she will be able to move a little more on her own so I can get her into a bed.

"I wish I could do more for you," I whispered as I sat on the floor with gauze, medical tape, alcohol swabs, and anti-bacterial cream scattered out in front of her.

Peeling back the gauze bandage on her shoulder, I cringed at the stitches that I could see. I remember her shudders and harsh whimpers as I pierced her skin with a needle closing the wound. I was so damn thankful I only had to stitch a few cuts on her body.

The bruises were lightening up a little, not that it helped. The dark purple marks had me originally fearing she was maybe internally bleeding.

I have been looking online for all the ways that I could medically help her. Short of taking her to the hospital, something I know I should have done and shame filled me. I didn't take her for more selfish reasons.

What if they asked too many questions? Zec would find me. But then there was a less selfish reason. What if the person or persons that did this found her there? She would be helpless. I knew the bad guys got to people in the hospital more than they should, and more than people knew.

Her lips moved, and air passed through her lips. I leaned over, trying to keep myself from touching or putting pressure on her. I was hoping to catch whatever she was saying.

"Thank you..." she whispered, before swallowing hard.

"Don't thank me. Anyone would have done this," it was a lie, and we both knew it.

Another swallow and then her lips were moving again.

"Did I bleed down there," her words were fearful.

My eyes darted to where she was talking about, and a frown forced a v between my eyes. Was she worried about getting blood on the furniture? Hell, she was bleeding everywhere.

Then it hit me. Oh god, my eyes widened so much they burned. I'm not sure if she did while they were doing whatever it was that they did. I knew for a fact she didn't while she was in my care.

"Sweetie, I don't know about before, but I can assure you that you haven't since I found you."

Her lips trembled, and I hated that I couldn't reassure her one hundred percent. My eyes once again went to her lower stomach, which was covered by the blanket. One of her hands were now pressed to her abdomen.

"I wish I could put clothes on you, but right now you need too much care."

She nodded slightly as tears tracked down her cheeks in clear heated rivers. Was the baby okay? Once again, I hated myself for not taking her to the hospital. I was no savior, I was just another monster.

Chapter 6

Ronnie

One Year and Five Months Ago.

I've been watching her as the months passed. The swell of her stomach always made me smile. All the bruises have faded, but her body had scars that would always be a reminder of what she went through.

I haven't asked her yet. I was waiting for her to come to me, but I couldn't wait any longer. I needed to know what we possibly faced.

I thought we had freedom and peace, but what if she was being hunted like me? We needed to get the fuck out of here if that was the case. We've been sitting ducks waiting to be picked off.

She was sitting on the very couch she fought to survive. Her eyes looked into mine, and the smile fell from her lips into a frown.

"Do we have to do this?" Her voice held pain, sorrow, and she shook with fear.

"Yes, not only will it help you, but I need to know what we're facing."

"Nothing. No one is looking for me," she said firmly.

"And you know this how?" I ask her, my voice held a bite to it that had her wincing. My heart tugged. I didn't want to talk to her like this.

"Because the only person who cared about me, only cared about her next high. Not the people who held me captive. They only wanted to hurt someone who couldn't care less what happened to me," she whispered, her voice started out strong, but the hitches and pain that laced through it had forced her to whisper the last eight words.

"Please, Maria? Talking about what happened to you will make you feel better," I begged her.

"Are you going to tell me what happened to you?" She asked, already knowing that I won't.

"That's what I thought," she sighed while standing up. Her over-sized stomach made the task harder than normal.

"I need to find a place to live."

My eyes went from her stomach to her face. She wanted to leave? I had more than enough space for her here.

"You don't need to leave," I tell her gently.

"It's not just for me but for my son."

"What about work? Money?" I asked her.

"I'll start looking. Its time I learn to stand on my own. We'll still be friends if I move out, right?"

My throat closed at the thought of being alone again. I didn't realize how alone I was until I found Maria.

"Always," I tell her all choked up.

Chapter 7

Gage

One Year and Three Months Ago.

It's been a few weeks since I've seen Crow. A few days after our last visit, I was transferred to another prison. I learned why really fucking quickly. The warden of the prison had blood knuckle fighting, and high-end bidders came to watch us fight in the cage.

Just a few select prisons participated, and I started to compose a list. When I got out of this shit hole, I was going to hunt down every motherfucking warden that participated.

These matches often got brutal. The bloodier, the better and some didn't make it. It was kill or be killed, but not all matches were that way.

To make shit worse, they weren't just killing each other in the cage. We had to watch our backs in our own damn cells.

The man in the cell next to mine convinced his cellmate to let him choke him. Thank fuck he wasn't my cellmate, the stupid fucker played right into the ice man's hands.

The guy convinced him that he would just choke until he passed out. The poor sucker thought of the big check he would get, and possible time being shaved off his sentence only to be choked over and over.

He kept going back to his body to make sure he wasn't breathing. That was Ice man's cellmate number two since I've been in this particular hell hole.

The last one he beat to death because his voice annoyed him. Ice Man put his body in his bed, and it took the guards all fucking day to figure out what the rest of us knew. He was dead.

Yet the ice man still got to stay here in low security. Not once was he thrown in the hole.

The men cheered and the stench of old and new blood perfumed the air. My opponent screamed as I pulled his hand back and snapped his wrist.

I was becoming someone that I didn't recognize. The thought of pain, the blood, and screams of others had excitement coursing through my blood humming like a drug.

This was an addiction at its best. I was no stranger to killing people. Fuck, I've tortured people with a smile on my face. But putting inmates against each other for rich fucks enjoyment, that was something else entirely.

My soul was darkening and turning black. Honestly, my heart was already black and hard as stone. I held the fucker that I was currently fighting by the hair on his head. My fist planted on his face repeatedly, and my knees pressed harder into the cold blood-soaked floor.

Fresh blood started to mix, again, with the old. His whimpers died down, and now there was nothing but the sound of flesh connecting with flesh. The noise of the betters hummed in the background.

This man now looked more like abused meat than human. He had a family, though, and I was going to kill him.

It was him or me, so I felt no remorse. Not one moment of could I do this. There was no hesitation. The fight started, and we tore at each other like animals who haven't fed in days.

The sound of the bell had me releasing a deep breath. My fingers unlatched from his blood-soaked hair, and he hit the ground with a wet squelch.

Sweat continued to drop down my forehead. I wiped it away with my hand, causing the blood to splatter on my face. The blood soaked my hands and spread over my face like some fucked up makeup.

I stood there and just looked down at the man I just killed. The inmate was, unfortunately, handed the short end of the deal when he found himself in this prison.

He died in a riot or so the report will read. He probably could blackmail the warden with some bullshit. But, the fucker had no chance.

Chapter 8

Ronnie

One Year and Three Months Ago.

It was no big secret that Maria had money saved. I knew that, but her struggle to live normal kept her working. She told me she liked to pretend that the money wasn't there.

I lifted another box and put it in the pickup truck that we rented. Maria didn't have much here, so there was no need for a U-Haul. The little house we found wasn't around here, but that was only a small relief.

There was going to come a time when I had to choose between running alone and telling her the truth and begging her to come with me. She was my family, my sister. My heart constricted as an image of Savanna filled my mind.

She was safe for now but for how long? I needed to get her out of there, but I haven't figured out how to do that yet. Hell, what if she didn't want to go? Life on the run was hard.

The sound of Shawn squawking had a small smile form on my face. I was smitten with the little cutie. The moment those beautiful eyes opened and met mine, I was lost.

"I'll get him," I told Maria.

Her eyes misted as she nodded. Whoever the father was, she still loved him. Whatever happened didn't destroy the feelings that swallowed her whole. Sometimes I could hear her crying as she begged for a second chance.

I was going to find out who he was as soon as I got her settled in her new place. I was going to share a small amount of my past in exchange for Shawn's father's identity. I needed to know why she refused to call him.

My heart swelled as I reached into the tiny car seat, which was a favorite of his. For some reason, Shawn slept better strapped into this thing then in a bed or anywhere else.

Unclipping the harness, I gently pulled his arms out of the straps. Then I slid one hand under his butt while the other went behind his head to cradle him.

Like a pro, I pulled him up and rested him against my shoulder, making soothing 'sssshhh' sounds near his ear. My cheek rested on his head, and his soft downy hair caressed my skin.

I remembered the first time I held this little boy. I was terrified I was going to break him. He was so small, and he weighed nothing. Only seven pounds and two ounces. The doctor had said that it was a good weight. He measured a twenty and a half inches long. Not that you would know that since his tiny legs stayed bent and close to his stomach.

"I've got you, sweet baby," I tell him as I rocked him back and forth over and over. My hips swayed while his head rested on my shoulder. The cries turned to little whimpers and then silence.

I continued to sway back and forth while my eyes closed. Memories came of me dancing in the garden along the stone path by our house. There were roses of all colors surrounding me.

In these moments, I felt like a fairy drifting through fairyland, a type of utopia. A place where I was free of the chain's that bound me. Even at seven, I knew what the future held for me.

I witnessed so many times where women were given to men of varying ages. Some even thirty years there senior. I knew my fate could be just as bad.

I remember as the years past, the understanding of what might happen to me in the future. The women who were married off would come to visit with their husbands as husks of their former selves.

Some were bruised while others looked empty. One stood out the most. She hated her life and refused to let it break her. My aunt was one hell of a woman.

The last time I had seen her, she grabbed my shoulders and told me to run. She said to find a way and get out of here. I was sixteen, and the reality of it all had already settled into my bones.

Her eyes were filled with fear. The man she was married to was forty years older than her. He was sick and sadistic.

I accidentally walked into a room and caught him choking her as he shoved his nasty thing down her throat. I gagged as tears filled my eyes. He wasn't even trying to hide how horrible he was. They were right there in the living room where others could watch. And they did watch.

Some sipped whiskey while others smiled as they took in the show. I couldn't see her like this, I needed to give her some dignity. So, I left.

I know she had seen me. Her fragile body shook as she leaned closer to me. Begging me to do what she said. I wanted the freedom she was talking about. The taste of freedom would be worth the death if I were caught.

I knew anything was better then what I had just seen. All I wanted was to be like other girls. Date boys and go to parties. Instead, I was wearing silky dresses and being shown off to all the gross men who were waiting for a chance to become my husband.

"You don't deserve this life, Roslin," she whispered as she pulled me to her. Her flowery scent filled my nose.

My arms instinctively wrapped around her waist. I loved her like she was my mother. Hell, she was more of a mother to me than my own.

My real mother saw me as a political advantage. She wanted the social standing that came with selling me off like a prized cow.

"You need to promise me, Roslin. Promise that you will get out of here and never look back," her grip tightened as she said it with a forceful voice. Something in me knew I was saying goodbye.

"I will," I tell her as my eyes started to sting.

"I love you, Roslin," she tells me as she cupped my cheeks. She then pressed her lips to my forehead.

"I love you too," I choked out past the lump in my throat.

I watched her walk away, and something in me died a little. She disappeared that night, and I heard whispers that she had run.

I prayed every night to a god that I wasn't sure was listening that she found her happy. The thought of her living a better life made the pain of her leaving easier.

They found her a week later. My mom was telling me that they tortured her for days before killing her. I remember my mom leaning in and telling me to take that as a warning. That I shouldn't try to do what she did, or I would end up just like her.

The problem was, I was now more determined than ever to get out of here. I promised a dead woman something. And I wasn't going to take it back. Even if I only got a few days of the free life, I would take it.

"That's everything," Maria's voice jarred me from the memories.

Another sadness filled me mixing with the brokenness of the past. I swallowed hard as I lowered Shawn back into his seat before strapping him in.

This wasn't a permeant goodbye, just an 'I'll see you soon.' I mean, I still had to help her unload the truck and everything.

"Alright," I tell her with a bright smile.

I was good at faking it. In reality, I wasn't happy about any of this.

Chapter 9

Ronnie

One Year Ago.

I thought we would get around to talking about our past at some point. But Maria got a job, and I became Shawn's babysitter, not that I was complaining. I loved this little boy like he was my own.

His little coos and giggles were infectious. Shawn had his own room here, and so did Maria. Even though she chose to move out, I wanted her to know that the door was always open. Tonight when she walked through it, I was determined that she wasn't leaving until we talked.

After Shawn went to bed, we will have a few drinks and figure shit out. I won't tell her about Zec, but I will share some of the milder shit. I wanted to know what had her running and why Shawn's father was MIA.

I felt like an asshole for cornering her like this, but we had to do it. No, I had to do this. So, I had a pot roast covered in carnitas sauce roasting in the crock pot.

Tonight, we will have baked potatoes stuffed with light butter, pulled pork, and some shredded cheddar cheese.

Chapter 10

Gage

One Year Ago.

Freedom had a smell to it. Like a fresh and sweet one, and I would have appreciated that months ago. Before I landed in that hell hole.

I went in a killer, willing to kill if I needed to, and came out a monster of destruction. Screams and blood made me happy.

How long has it been since I smiled? Weeks? Fuck, my last match was almost a month ago. I tried to keep myself busy with the thought of my freedom. I was hoping to keep my sanity, but I lost that after my twentieth fight.

Killing over and over and beating a man to a bloody death started to feel more like an air freshener than the clawing stench it was. Honestly, I had stripped away what made me human.

Sociopaths, shit I could relate. I felt nothing unless I was breaking bones and watching the light leave their almost completely closed eyes. You know, that glassy, cloudy look that filled them moments after their death.

Crow was leaning against his bike, and mine was a few feet away. That was it, no one else was here. Something had changed in him too. This coldness had taken him a few months after my transfer.

I asked what the fuck was going on. I guess his old lady left without a word, disappearing as if she was never there at all.

A small gust of wind blew my hair to the left. The whole inch that it was. While I was in there, I kept it shaved. When men realized it was do or die, they pulled out their inner bitch.

Hair grabbing was a go-to move. So, shaving it meant no one could latch onto my head and control my movements. I had a whole new respect for women with that move.

"Never thought you'd drag your ass out here, I've been waiting for two fucking hours," Crow's voice was loud.

The area around us was devoid of any houses. No one wanted to live near a prison, and every prisoner was inside waiting for the moment they could roam around the outside.

"Had a few things to clear up," I tell him with a shrug.

I wasn't telling anyone what went down in this place and not because the warden gave me some pussy warning about the consequences of spreading the word.

I tuned him out as soon as he started telling me that I needed to keep my mouth shut. There wasn't a fucking thing he could say that would scare me.

"Are we going to stand here all fucking day or can we get our ass's moving? I need a beer," the words were harsh, and I expected Crow to say or do something to put me in my place. Instead, he laughed a hollow dark laugh and climbed on his bike.

Something tells me we both went dark. That we lost ourselves in the sea of blackness that lived in us all. I let mine consume me and fuck maybe Crow did too.

Chapter 11

Ronnie

Present Day.

It's been a year since I asked Maria what happened. Her eyes watered as she told me about the love she found and the loss as she watched him with another woman. She told me who he really was and what he did.

Honestly, if I were normal and not raised in the nightmare that I called my previous life, I would have been terrified.

When she told me about being chained to the floor over the very man who didn't want her, my heart broke, and tears filled my eyes.

She knew he wasn't going to save her. She endured hell alone while waiting for death, and she didn't see any escape or savior.

The cup hit the table hard, which caused me to jump slightly in my chair. Maria disappeared with Crow leaving me here in this room full of bikers.

I sipped the whiskey while I looked around. Every step that I've made brought me here to this moment, to this place, and to this dick face currently staring at me.

Said dick face was the only one who brought me a drink. Those dark eyes spoke of torture, pain, and dark pleasures.

Have you ever had that tingle of awareness? When the hairs stand up on your body. The desire to be closer and yet run further away from whatever it was whispering over your body.

Gage was that exact thing for me. This deep need to lean in and the rooted fear to run. Everything about him pissed me off for no logical reason.

I resisted the urge to cover myself and throat punch him at the same time. His penetrating stare stripped away layers, leaving a coldness in their wake.

Fuck sipping this bitter shit, throwing my head back I drank the contents in the glass in one quick swallow.

I winced at the burn, but I needed the pain. You see, I did this. I brought us here. She thought she was running because of her sister and that she brought me into this nightmare.

My heart clenched, she was so wrong. I did this. I dragged her into my past. They had finally caught up to me.

My breath hitched. I saved Maria only to kill her. Sure, she was still living, but for how long? Maybe I should go. Call Zec and give myself over to him.

I could barter my life, my freedom, my soul for theirs. My eyes locked on Gage's and he knew. I could read it on his face. He knew something wasn't right with me.

I hated myself a little more. Darkness spread through me when I didn't save Zec's wife, and it continued to spread through me. I was a fool to think that saving Maria could change my past.

I was condemned the moment that I took a breath in this life. My life was never my own, and I'm my own bid for freedom. I was destroying other people, and I was so selfish.

Deep down, I knew this man right here was going to be the one to turn me over. He was going to take me to them like the executioner I could see lurking in his eyes.

"Staring is rude, you know," I tell him with a smile.

"I'm more than rude, and you're more than a pretty face."

He had me there. But at the same time, he didn't. In my family, I was nothing but a pretty face. Here, I was the destruction of all that I came in contact with.

"Do you use that line often? What's the success rate for that big guy?"

I was goading him. Trying to draw him away from the scent before he went in for the kill. This crazy fucker right here would probably kill me.

Just lean forward and get a little taste of those sexy as fuck lips, the thought had my breath stilling in my lungs.

Where the fuck did that come from? Not once in all my damn life have I wanted to kiss another person, let alone a man.

Well, except for Shawn, of course. I couldn't help but want to kiss his chubby little cheeks. His little giggles warmed my soul.

A red claw-tipped hand slithered up his chest from behind. My eyes remained on that hand. Something in me wanted to grab it and squeeze the tiny wrist until bones rubbed together and toss it away.

Something dark swirled inside of me when a scantily clad woman stepped out from behind him. Her blonde hair streaked with brown had my eyes lowering to slits.

I wanted to snatch every one of those strands from her head. I wanted to make her cry and tell her to keep her dainty STD covered hand off my man.

My man? Oh god, I was losing it. I was cracking down the middle. Something in my brain had snapped since Gage was not mine. Fuck, I met him only a few hours ago or was it yesterday? I was losing time. How long have I sat here?

I was on my twelfth drink?

With that thought, my stomach dipped and soured. Bile filled my throat, leaving a burning sensation with each inch it conquered.

Standing, I tilted, and everything rushed to my head. I needed the bathroom, and I also need the room to still.

Something cool latched onto the back of my neck. It relieved some of the heat that was overwhelming my skin.

"Easy," Gage ordered.

"Don't tell me what to do," I choked out.

It was coming on fast. That bathroom was my lighthouse in the foggy night. It was my hope of relief. I swayed as I tried to take a step. That hand I thought was so wonderful tightened.

"Let me go before I make you regret it," in my head, I sounded strong and confident, but what came out was garbled and weak.

"If I let you go your face will be meeting the floor," he says with a shrug.

The woman was still holding onto him like some sort of life sucking octopus or leach. Leach lips. Laughter tried to come out. Instead, my eyes watered.

"I need the bathroom, let me go before I take that sex appeal down multiple levels."

His laughter was rich and deep. It pulled something deep inside of me. The vomit, it had to be that.

"Feeling a little green?" He was no longer Mr. Hottie.

"Seriously, Gage. My stomach is coming up my throat, and I don't know how long I can keep it where it belongs." Sobering up was happening way faster than it should.

Seeing this woman, his hand on my body, combined with my traitorous thoughts had me draining the liquor and making life reappear.

Shaking off his hold, I speed walked to the bathroom. I didn't look back, I kept my head high and my dignity as much intact as I could.

The bathroom swallowed me as the door closed with a click. Tears filled my eyes for a different reason. That vomit I had been fighting hit me like a runaway train.

Dropping to the cold tile floor, I leaned into the toilet and empty the contents of my stomach. After what felt like an eternity, I was left shaking and weak. If only I could purge my sins just as easily as I purged the alcohol from my body.

Chapter 12

Gage

Present Day.

Fucking anything that walked was what I did. Emotions were never apart of the equation before prison. I would flash women a smile and maybe even give them some sweet words. Now, I fucked them and walked away, closing the door behind me before I even zipped up my fly.

Yet the women kept coming for more. Some of them had some fucked-up notion that they could tame me and that I would claim them as my old lady.

Old ladies were for others. There was nothing left of me to give or share. They needed feelings, and I lost those in the pit.

"You stare at her much longer, she might take a restraining order out on your ass," Crow laughed as he sipped his beer.

I couldn't take my eyes off her. There was something not right with her. She should be terrified. Especially in a place filled with bikers running from the mob.

I watched as she casually drank and watched the people around her. She had this look in her eyes. It told me that she had seen more than most.

Like a cat, she probably had multiple lives. Crow told me that Ronnie saved Maria's life. There was something about this whole fucked up situation, and it involved her.

"She's not right," I tell him.

"Neither are you brother," Crow reminded me.

I looked at him. His eyes had lost some of the coldness, but the darkness remained. Maria had lived in hell, and Crow hadn't been there for her or their son. That shit ate a man alive.

"She's involved in this somehow," I tell him.

"Yeah, she's in it with Maria," Crow said harshly. Emotions were riding him hard. Something I haven't seen in him in a long fucking time.

"I'm not going to stop watching her," I tell him with a shrug.

I'm going to figure this out. Both of them put our club in jeopardy, and only one of them was an old lady. The other was just some chick dragging destruction behind her like a puppy on a leash.

"Club meeting in ten," Crow announced.

I rolled my shoulders and drank my beer in a few deep swallows. Ronnie froze for a moment and then continued drinking as her eyes scanned the room.

Oh, sweetheart, you just showed me there was definitely something not right with you and Crow caught it too. I could see the way he tensed.

"We'll talk about it in the room," he tells me coldly.

"Maria must know something," I tell him.

"If she does, she would have told me," his tone darkened telling me to tread carefully.

"She may not know that she knows it," my tone was cold.

He nodded his head as his eyes lock on both women. Maria joined Ronnie at the table. They laugh and smile as they talk.

Something made me want to touch her, hold her, keep her close, and protect her. Feelings I've never felt for anyone swirled inside of me mixing with numb darkness.

Fuck! What the fuck was wrong with me? Slamming the empty bottle down, I follow Crow. I watch as all our brothers settle in their seats.

"Maria brought some trouble to the club," Crow announced.

No one had the balls to say anything. I know what most of them were thinking, kick her ass out.

"She's my old lady, and he's my son. You know how this shit works," Crow growls.

Lincoln shifts in his seat. Something about him has been bothering me for a while now. But his reaction to Maria had warnings screaming through my head.

"She's been gone a long time," Lincoln comments.

My eyes are glued to him now. He was another that I needed to watch closely. He had it out for Maria and has since she walked through those doors. I also took note of the way he looked at Ronnie.

The thought of him touching her in any way had me wanting to gut him from groin to throat. No one touched what's mine, and Ronnie was mine.

What the fuck? She was an enemy until proven innocent. She was not mine. An image of him running his fingers through her long brown locks and the way her lips would part and the moan that would escape had me gripping the edge of the table.

I glared at Lincoln. I would kill him, tear him limb from limb. Crow was still talking, and I should be listening, but all I could think about was killing this piece of shit sitting at our table. I wanted to rip his spine out through his throat.

He was my brother, and he was my enemy. I knew one thing, Lincoln was going to die. He just didn't know it yet.

Chapter 13

Ronnie

Present Day.

Pretending was exhausting. I was pretending to be some free-spirited badass. Although, the worst was pretending that none of this was my fault. The only thing I wasn't pretending about was how much I cared for Maria and Shawn.

The chair in front of me scrapes against the cold hard cement floor. My eyes lock on the blond with the long claw-like red nails who was climbing Gage like a spider monkey in heat last night.

"Whatever you're thinking about, you can just give it up," the blond tells me with a smug smile.

This was beyond hilarious! She had no clue what I was thinking. I wondered if she even had enough brain cells to stem together a real thought.

"And what am I thinking about?"

Her green eyes narrow, and her lips pursed. Huh, I could almost see the wheels grinding and the smoke billowing out.

"Gage, of course," she says it like that's all I could possibly be thinking about.

"Sweetheart, I think about more things than the dick I want between my legs," my tone was condescending, and by the looks of it, I completely lost her.

"See, you admit it. You want Gage," she insinuated each word with her claw-like fingers.

Sighing, I sat further back in my seat. Was she for real? I was literally blown away by this woman. I had more shit to worry about than who Gage was fucking.

The thought of him fucking her or anyone else was like a curved dagger in my chest. The anger at him and myself had me lashing out at the poor dimwitted woman.

"I've got a very serious question for you," I tell her once again as I lean forward.

She leans in too. Her eyes are still narrowed as if she was trying to intimidate me.

"Better not be about Gage."

"Oh, sweetheart, it's not. Trust me," I give her my biggest smile.

She nods, and somewhere in her little brain, I think she believes that she won some victory.

"How the hell do you wipe your ass with those things?" I mean really, the damn things are like an inch long and pointed at the end.

"You're disgusting, and for your information, I do it just fine!" she screams as she stands up and walks away.

Laughter fills my chest, and it escapes in painful bouts. I watch her walk off with watery eyes.

"Are you tormenting people?" Maria asks as she sits down, holding a squirming Shawn.

"Not really," I tell her with a shrug.

Her smile is wide and real. Something I've only seen when she looks at her child but even then, the sadness lingered in her eyes. Today that was missing.

"Will you hold Shawn? I need to get him something to eat."

As if she needed to ask. Reaching out, I pull the squirming child to my chest. Lifting him up, I blow a raspberry onto his truck covered onesie.

His little giggles warmed me. So, I tickle and make funny faces.

"You're good with him," Gage's deep voice startles me.

"Thanks, I think," I wasn't sure if that was just a compliment or a complement combined with an insult.

"Do you have kids?" he asks the question as if he was talking about the weather.

"If I had kids they would be here," I snap at him. Why the fuck would I leave them alone and only hide myself. Especially in this place, hmm, what's going on?

"I'm just trying to figure you out," he shrugs as if he didn't just give me an imaginary slap.

Terror filled my blood. No one could know about me. When and if I shared it, it will depend on there being no other choice.

"There's not much to know," I give him a shrug of indifference.

"Everyone has a past. Boyfriends? Husbands? Lovers?" he growls.

Almost husband, yes, but never a lover or boyfriend. But he's right, everyone has a past, and if I want to blend in, I needed to share some shit. I'll just keep it as close to the truth as possible. Lies are hard to keep. One lie always leads to another and then another, and before you know it, you don't know what you lied about.

"I grew up in a strict family. No men allowed until I was married," I shrug.

It's the truth to a point. Gage's eyes darken, and something sparks there.

"Where did you live?"

He was like a fucking bloodhound, or more appropriately, a hell hound.

"A long way from here, and I don't intend to go back. I left because I didn't want to fall into their plans, and I want a life of my own," I tell him coldly.

I left out that they would never accept me back, not really. If they did catch up to me, I would be living in a hell the devil himself would find terrible.

Screaming came from the other room. Maria was screaming, and something in me snapped. I was holding Shawn close to me while I moved as fast as I could. But not fast enough to hurt him.

The scene that was playing out in front of me had tears in my eyes, my heart shattering, and my world falling apart. Maria kept going on about someone in this place wanting her dead. The very one who handed her over to those men.

I stood there, helpless as my best friend fought terror, and the memories were trying to drag her into the pit of hell. Crow was holding her as she clawed and tried to climb over his shoulder.

She begged me to get Shawn out of there and save him. Gage pushed in behind me. I was ready to run even if everything in me screamed not to leave her behind. The baby was all that mattered.

"Don't even think about it," he whispered in my ear.

I shuddered. We were all trapped. Even though I was being forced to stay and was even being gently prodded down the hallway, I wanted to sink into the man's arms and beg him to save me from what was to come.

Soon I would need to make a choice. A choice I knew deep down I had already made. I was going to go home. I needed to save my friend and this child. I had to consider my nephew.

But before I did, there was something my body screamed for, and my heart begged for. I wanted to know what it felt like to be loved, even if it wasn't real. I wanted to feel Gage everywhere.

Chapter 14

Gage

Present Day.

Lincoln was a trader, and that's all I know. Soon I will be able to give the piece of shit some gifts because I'm generous as fuck.

Ronnie looked at me like she needed me to pull her close and contain whatever was haunting her from escaping. I wasn't a hero, even if I wanted to give in and do just that.

I should want to be as far from her as possible. The more I'm around her, the more I want and need to be closer. To touch her and keep her.

"I've got this deal with him," Weston spits.

I look back at the bed that Ronnie and Maria are laying on. They are on their sides with Shawn in the middle of them, sleeping. Crow dropped Maria off an hour after everything went down while Weston collected Lincoln and put him in the basement.

Closing the door, I made my way to the basement. Crow was already there standing in front of Lincoln who was strung up like fresh kill.

His shoes, socks, and shirt have all been removed, leaving him in jeans. One of his eyes was already swollen shut. Crow was pacing back and forth, his hands were clenching and unclenching as he went.

"My fucking brother! I protected you, paid you, fed you, and gave you a roof over your fucking head. I gave you purpose, you piece of shit!" Crow shouted.

Stepping closer, I lean down so I could get a closer look at Lincoln's face. His head was hanging low with blood dripping onto the cold stained floor.

"Why? Why the fuck would you do that to me, to her?" Crow demanded.

"That fucking cow was in my way. You were never supposed to be president, that was mine!" Lincoln screamed through swollen lips.

Every muscle in Crow's body stiffened. He froze mid-step and turned to look at Lincoln.

"You? This was never going to be yours. You fucking handed over my old lady for this patch? You turned trader for a fucking patch?"

The calmness that settled over Crow screamed that there wasn't going to be any mercy. This fucker was family. My instincts to kill him on the spot. Now, I wished I could do the job myself. I needed to satiate this blood lust, this hunger.

"I would have given you a chance to fight in the cage, but you tried to tear us apart. I won't give you any mercy," Crow snarls as he turns and grabs a kabob skewer.

The long thin metal had been welded together with about three other skewers to give it the strength needed to pierce flesh.

Blood poured from his armpit as the metal went through the sensitive fatty flesh. Lincoln screamed over and over as Crow tore into him.

"You're going to regret this," Lincoln choked.

"Can't fucking hear you!" Crow shouts as he ran the knife over one of Lincoln's nipples.

The room was filled with the coppery scent of blood.

"I told them. They're coming," Lincoln laughed.

Crow snarled and slit his throat. Blood ran like a river down his chest as Lincoln jerked over and over, and gurgling filled the room.

"What the fuck was he talking about?" Knox asked.

"Just running his fucking mouth. Hoping to walk out of this alive. Probably would have offered some shit up if we let him go," Crow shrugs.

Blood coated him like a second skin. His cut was draped over the stool in the corner.

"Go get a shower, prez," I tell him.

"Yeah, I don't want to scare the old lady. I'll grab your cut," Knox tells him.

As Crow starts to walk away, he looks at me. The darkness had risen in me. I needed a fight, and I needed one bad.

"I'll set up a match tonight," Crow tells me as he walks out of the room.

For the first time in what felt like weeks, I felt a smile stretch over my face.

Chapter 15

Maria

Present Day.

I had sinned. There were so many things that I needed to atone for, and it weighed me down. I was broken inside, but Maria and Shawn were like Band-Aids trying desperately to hold me together.

I needed to tell her the truth of who I was and what I did. Looking down at my hands, they look just like they always have, but inside I knew they were rotting, just like I was.

"Keep drinking like that, and you're going to pass the fuck out," Gage's deep hypnotic voice washed over me.

Another thing in my life that I had to atone for. The need that I felt for him. The darkness in him pulled the darkness in me, like two oversized magnets.

"That's kind of the point," I tell him with a self-deprecating laugh.

"Whatever the fuck has you sinking, don't let it drown you," he tells me quietly.

He sounded almost like he cared. For a moment, my heart swelled. The stupid organ didn't know that Gage was off limits. It didn't deserve what it so actively pumped for.

Giving in to it, even for a moment, would be signing his death certificate.

"I've been drowning. You get used to it," I smile my big fake smile.

I wait for him to say something so I could come up with some witty reply. Instead, he just stared at me like he could see into my very center and rip my secrets out.

"Don't you have some blond needing your attention," I sounded jealous enough that I feared my eyes had turned green and my hair was cackling in some electrical wave.

The very thought of that had me laughing. Even though the thought of Gage with the blond dug a deep hollow pit in me, the image of me looking like some crazy avenging witch was too much for my drunk brain.

My eyes widened as Gage leaned in close. I could feel the heat radiating off his body. His fingers pulled the hair away from my ear and draped it over my shoulder.

"I have a fight in a few minutes, but after that, your mine," his hot breath filled my ear, causing shivers to shake my body.

Oh fuck. Swallowing another shot, I watched as he walked away. You were just reminding yourself that being with him was a bad fucking idea. Now you're ready to just surrender?

Why can't you have just one night? Isn't that what freedom is? My mind whispered.

I was free, but for how long? My brain must have known how this was going to end, because why not have what I wanted before I had to die?

Chapter 16

Ronnie

Present Day.

I could hear the screams and cheers from here. A part of me wanted to see Gage fight, the other didn't want to witness the darkness that I could see surrounding him. I felt the need to set him free. I wondered was he winning?

My mind was at war with itself. I wanted to get closer to Cage. I wanted to feel his body against mine. I needed to feel his lips and his hands, but I also wanted to run as fast and as far as this building would let me.

Instead of doing either of those things, I was once again sitting at the table. I feel like I could almost call this place home. So, I drank.

I knew deep down I was going to Gage's room tonight and let him do all the filthy things I've dreamed about since I've met him. I shouldn't, but then what did I have to lose? My life? That was already gone.

"Lost in your thoughts again?" Maria's sweet voice pulled me from the darkness that wanted to pull me in.

"You know how it is, life and all," I tell her with a small 'who gives a shit' shrug.

I wanted to grab her and pull her into a hug and whisper all my sins. Tell her about Zec, and why he was really after her.

"Everything will be okay."

Her small hand rubbed up and down my back in a soothing gesture. Guilt filled me. I should tell her the truth, but would she hate me if she knew everything?

"We need to talk."

There was no way around this. The guilt of my life was choking me. My eyes locked onto the drink in front of me. I couldn't stand to look her in the eye. Not when I tell her everything.

"I'm here for you," she again rubs my back as she whispers those comforting words.

Except they were no comfort for me. They made my guilt unbearable, and my lies painful.

"It's about everything going on," I tell her. I couldn't look into her eyes, even though I tried to lift my head. Self-hatred was a powerful thing.

"Come on," Gage's dark voice pushed through the cloud of pity and concern.

I looked around and realized Maria was gone. Was she ever really there? Was the poison that was rotting away in me making me see things?

I looked at the seat next to me. Maria wasn't there, hell the chair was pushed in as if no one had been there. Go figure, I finally get the lady balls to tell her, and she was a figment of my imagination.

Taking a deep breath, I finally look at Gage. There was a cut on his left eyebrow, a bruise under his eye, and his lip was split.

"Looks like that hurt," I say in shock. I mean, with all the shouting I kind of expected more. Like a broken nose and well maybe a few broken ribs.

Just to be sure, I leaned forward and poked him hard in the ribs.

"If they were broken that would have hurt like a bitch," he grumbled.

"Well, fucking excuse me for showing concern," I snap.

"If that was a concern, remind me to never get too close if I'm seriously hurt," he laughs.

"Come on warrior woman," he laughs as he holds out his hand.

I smile, despite everything. I need this. I need Gage, and for the second time in my life, it was purely selfish. I placed my hand in his, letting him pull me to my feet. It was time to truly be free.

Chapter 17

Ronnie

Present Day.

The trip to his room was a blur of motion. Probably because he said I was moving too slow and he literally threw me over his shoulder, caveman style.

Then I was free falling for what felt like forever as he tossed me on the bed. I bounced three times before settling, and this caused a fit of giggles.

"I always wondered what it would feel like to be on a trampoline," I tell no one.

I thought for sure he would press me on it. I mean, who hasn't been on a trampoline, at least once in their lives? Maybe not as a kid, but sure as fuck as an adult.

The bed dipped under his weight, and then he was pulling my clothes from my body like I was on fire and he was trying to save me.

I thought this would be a slow affair. You know, one piece of clothing here, some heavy petting then another piece of clothing. But to my utter drunken surprise, the man was naked and now so was I.

"Fuck, you're beautiful," he growls.

I don't want to hear the flattery. I'm sure all the other girls have. I just wanted to feel free. I wanted the guilt and pain to be gone, at least for a little while.

Leaning forward, I wrap my arms around his neck and pull him to me. My lips press to his, gently, and the heat filled my body as we kissed.

There was this burning need inside of me. The more Gage's lips caressed mine, the more I wanted. His calloused hand moved slowly up my inner thigh. Leaving a trail of tingles.

The closer he got to my pussy, the more my hips lifted, and I pulled him closer. I needed him so badly, it hurt.

"So, fucking wet and tight," he groaned.

His finger slipped inside of me. Thrusting gently as his tongue slid past my lips. It was too much and at the same time, not enough.

"God, please," I begged.

Then, another finger joined the first. Gage was stretching me, and there was a hint of pain mixing with the pleasure. Another rock of my hips.

"Not god, baby," he chuckled.

My head dropped back as moans passed my lips. The things I was feeling should be illegal. His thumb brushed my clit, and I was lost. My nails sunk into his skin as I screamed. My hips rocked uncontrollably as I came hard.

Gage's lips crashed back onto mine as his cock nudged my opening. One hand slid under my ass, lifting me as the other slid into my hair, fisting the brown locks and holding me in place.

Moans poured from me as his hard dick slid up and down my slit. He coated himself in my juices, once again, lining up with the opening of my pussy.

My nails dug into his back as he pushed forward. Forcing his thick cock into my tight virgin pussy. One inch at a time.

It was too much. Gage kept pushing forward, and I felt like I was ripping in two.

"You're too big," I cry, trying to scoot away. Although Gage's arm was holding me, and it made that impossible.

"Stop fighting me," he growls.

"I'm not fighting, you just aren't going to fit!" I cry.

Another inch of his fat cock and I swear I could feel every vein, every throb, and every ridge. He kept ramming his oversized cock into my pussy as I fought to breathe.

It was too much. I pushed at Gage's shoulders again, trying to wiggle out from under him. Then he leaned forward using his weight and forced more into me.

Just when I thought I was going to die, he pushed through my barrier. Pain exploded as he bottomed out, and my head flung back as I cried out. I felt more shoving, and I needed him out of me.

"Shhh, baby. I promise this will feel fucking amazing," he whispered into my ear.

Tears fell from my eyes as my body stretched to its limits and fought to accept him. Sweet kisses along my neck had my stomach fluttering.

After what felt like an eternity, the pain turned to a dull ache. Then, the beginning of pleasure started to come back. My pussy loosened and tightened on him as I thought of that orgasm that he just gave me.

"Fuck!" he growled, and then he was moving. In and out, and in long, steady, powerful thrusts. Stretching me and filling me over and over.

"Sweetest fucking pussy," he groaned as he slammed into me harder, hitting my womb over and over. Another orgasm was building.

My pussy tightened as he pushed into me with short, hard thrusts hitting my clit with every return. Wetness gushed around his cock, electing another groan from him.

"You're going to take all of me," he growled as he pulled out and flipped me over. My knees hit the bed, and before my arms could stop my chest from hitting the bed, he was plowing back into me.

From this position, he was sinking in deeper, and his thrusts were harder. Those big calloused hands held my hips, forcing me to take every inch of his massive cock.

He was powering into me so hard that we were sliding up the bed.

"Take it all. I'm going to own this tight, wet pussy," Gage groaned and growled as he thrust in and out, using my body any way he wanted. Forcing me to take what he wanted to give.

Then it hit me like a fucking wrecking ball. Slamming into and destroying me as my orgasm literally took my breath away.

Every muscle in my body locked up, my pussy clamped down on his thick, heavily-veined dick while my body pulled the orgasm from him.

Gage pulled my hips towards him as he pushed into me hard and fast. The head of his cock continued to press into my womb as he filled me to the brim with hot jets of cum.

"My pussy," he growled, his fingers were digging into my hair and pulling my head back. "You're mine."

He stayed deep inside of me, holding my hair for what felt like an eternity before I responded, "Yours."

Chapter 18

Gage

Present Day.

I wanted her for a quick fuck, and that was it. I was like I sunk into nirvana. She had a fucking perfect pussy. The thought of someone else touching her had me claiming her.

Ronnie was my old lady. As of last night, when I came so fucking hard, I thought my balls would never empty. Especially when I realized that I was the first man to have her pussy.

Sliding from the bed, I smiled as she grumbled. I needed to tell my brothers that she was mine. Also, Ronnie and I needed to talk about whatever she was hiding. But for now, I had shit to do. Even though I wanted to sink back into her pussy and make her scream my name.

After last night, I knew she was sore. There was no fucking today and possibly not tomorrow. That left talking, something she was going to do a whole lot more of.

Pulling on my cut, I made my way out of the room. The text I got last night, after Ronnie fell asleep, told me there was a meeting this morning at nine am.

The door beside mine opened, and Weston stumbled out. His bloodshot eyes met mine. I hated fucking meeting early, and I guess I wasn't the only one.

"Fuck, man, my head is killing me," Weston grumbled.

I laughed and slapped him on the back. Normally this early morning shit had me ready to take someone's head off, but not today. Shit, for the first time since I left that fucking hellhole, I wasn't stuck in constant bloodlust.

Walking into the room, I looked around at my brothers. They were all sitting at the table wearing frowns. Not one single coffee cup to be seen.

"No coffee?"

"No, we all just got the fuck up at the ass crack of dawn," Weston grumbled.

Crow frowns at him before turning to the rest of us. Once my ass hit the chair, the meeting started. I should feel flattered that he waited that damn long. From the look on his face, he was impatient as fuck.

"We have some shit headed our way, and we need to get prepared," Crow announces.

What the fuck now? We already had to deal with the fucking Albanian mob.

"Maria says her sister is out there somewhere and that the Albanians are searching for her," Crow continues.

What the fuck does her sister have to do with this shit? I say hand the junkie over and call it a fucking day.

"If all they want is her sister, let's find the sister and present her with a bow."

Crow looks at me, and something tells me he had thought the same thing.

"She's my old ladies' sister," he sighed.

"Yeah and she turned on her fucking sister," Weston growls.

"Can you honestly look Maria in the eyes after we hand her sister over to those fucking savages?" Knox asks us all.

"I can," I shrug when they all look at me like I lost my fucking mind.

"We need to prepare before they get here. Fuck, maybe we can work out some deal," Crow sighs as he rubs at his temples.

"Yeah, the sister," I snap.

What the fuck is wrong with them. Can't they see the only solution was to hand over what they wanted and move the fuck on? We didn't need a war with those crazy fucks.

"Prepare for war," Crow announces, ignoring my last comment.

"Well if that's all, I wanted to say that Ronnie's mine," my tone left no room for argument.

Crow looked at me and frowned. And Weston all but fell out of his chair.

"What the fuck?" Knox says.

I glare at all my brothers. What the fuck was their problem?

"One time in the sack and you're claiming her? Fuck, maybe I should give her a try," Weston laughs.

Pulling my arm back, I slam my fist into his face and watch as he once again falls out of his chair. This time, the chair went with him.

"That's my old lady. Respect and reverence when talking about her," I snarl at him.

"Anyone got something to say about her?" I ask my brothers, coldly. When no one said anything, I settled back into my chair more comfortably.

"Just get ready," Crow sighs again as he stands up.

The rest of my brothers, I was sure, shuffled out in search of coffee. As much as I wanted coffee, there was something else that I wanted more.

Chapter 19

Ronnie

Present Day.

Rolling over, I reach across the bed to look for Gage only to find the bed empty and the sheets cold. When did he leave? Should I leave?

Why the fuck should I stay? If he wanted me here, he would have said so. Sighing, I sit up and slowly scoot to the edge of the bed.

Just because he said I was his, he didn't really mean anything. I could chalk it up to being in the moment. Grabbing my jeans and underwear, I slowly pull them up my legs and over my hips. Winching as my sore pussy pressed into the mattress.

As soon as my shirt cleared my head and fluttered around my waist, the door opened. Shit, I was hoping to be out of here to avoid being thrown the fuck out.

The walk of shame was only worse when you get tossed out of the room. Placing both hands over my face, I rub it in frustration.

"Where are you going?" Gage's deep voice filled the quiet room.

The question had my hands dropping and my eyes locking onto his. Was this a joke? Was he fucking with me right now?

"I was leaving before I could be tossed out," I tell him with a self-deprecating laugh. I figured I should be honest. It's not like I could humiliate myself any more than I have.

"Who the fuck's tossing you out?" he asks coldly.

"Ugh, you?" My question was filled with the confusion that I was feeling.

"I told you last night, you're mine," he says, sounding a little disgruntled.

Awkwardly, I sat down on the bed and tried to fight my wince. Shit, I felt like someone took a battering ram to me. Then again, Gage's cock could probably be considered a battering ram.

"I was hoping to slip back into bed with you."

I laugh, yeah that wasn't happening. "Sorry buddy, but that's closed for construction. Seems someone broke it last night."

The laugh that fell from those perfect lips had my heart clenching in my chest. Shit, I was so fucked literally and figuratively.

"I'm hungry," I tell him just as my stomach growls.

"Come on sweetness, I'll feed that monster before it commits a crime," he laughs as I punch him in the arm.

My chest pinched. I could fall in love with this man. *You already have,* and the thought was terrifying.

Chapter 20

Ronnie

Present Day.

Guilt was like a heavy stone around my neck. It was so damn heavy, my back hurt. Maria sat across from me, and her eyes were sad. I hated myself for not telling her everything.

"I wish I could tell him to just give them my sister," Maria whispers.

Hate was a strong thing, and self-hatred was the worst. Sighing, I grab Maria and pull her into an awkward hug over the table. After I tell her this, I know she may walk away without looking back. Hell, I wouldn't blame her, but I couldn't sit back and let her blame herself not anymore.

"I need to tell you something. Please don't hate me," I tell Maria while grabbing her hand. Tears started to fill my eyes.

"Ronnie?" she whispers, "I could never hate you."

Oh god, I so hope that was true. Swallowing the lump that was choking me, I spilled my secrets.

"It's Rosaline," I tell her, which was the first of many confessions.

"Huh?"

"My name is Rosaline. I was born Rosaline." I choke on my last name, it wasn't coming and fuck it. Truthfully, it wasn't all that important in the grand scheme of things.

"I don't understand."

Closing my eyes, I let the past swallow me. I thought of the memories and every moment I had with Maria and Shawn. Which was soon to be demolished by what I can't change.

"I was born into the Albanian mob. My father agreed to marry me off to the head of the family. He was a monster, hell he was viler than that. He may even be the devil himself and his brother the prince of hell."

I can't look at her. My eyes are glued to the table, and I take a small comfort in the fact her hand is still in mine.

"I wanted nothing but freedom. I was trapped in a life I didn't want. I was to be married to a man who committed some atrocious crimes to his own wife. He killed her so he could have me."

Admitting that was something I thought I could never do. I was the reason a woman was dead.

"I stole money from my father and ran. I found you a few months after I left. Sometimes I think you would have been better off if I had dropped you at a hospital. But I was worried you could be like me and running for your very life."

The silence was killing me, but I didn't let it stop the flow of words. The gut-wrenching truth as it poured out like an unhealing wound.

"I know my fate if I was found. I would be made an example of. I was never going to stay in one place too long, but I couldn't leave you. I should have, you wouldn't have been put into this mess. It's me they want, not you."

The hand that I was so relieved to feel slipped away, and so did another piece of my soul.

"So, my sister…"

Looking up at her, I made sure she can see the truth in my face as I say the words.

"She did turn you in, I can't change that. I'm sorry, but Zec is after me, not you."

I wait for her to rail, scream, anything. Again, I look away. Her carefully blank face cut into me in ways I never thought possible.

"You saved me and stayed in one place for me?" she asks.

"I understand if you need to turn me over. I know you must hate me. Wait, what?" I was choking on the words only to fall into confusion.

"You said you needed to stay on the move, and yet you set down roots for me?" Her voice was low, giving nothing away.

"Yes, I couldn't leave you." I gave a shrug as if it was that simple.

"Shit," Maria whispers.

Closing my eyes, I think of all the things that were about to happen. Maria would surely tell the guys, and I would soon find myself in front of Zec. I couldn't blame them really.

"Crow," Maria says quickly.

My eyes snap open and lock on Gages who was literally standing over Maria's shoulder. From the look on his face, he heard everything.

"We need to talk," Crow tells Maria then he looks at Gage. "Call a meeting. I want to talk to everyone in an hour."

Without even looking at me, he grabs Maria's hand gently and pulls her to her feet. Out of the corner of my eyes, I saw that she disappeared from view. Honestly, I was afraid to take my eyes off Gage.

"Come on," his voice was quiet with not a hint of what he was feeling or thinking.

Swallowing, I allow him to pull me from the table, and in the direction of his room. Letting him wasn't an option, it was going to happen whether I let it or not.

Chapter 21

Ronnie

Present Day.

I expected Gage to be angry. Instead, he pushed me towards the bed and demanded that I strip. Quickly. So, I slowly unbuttoned my pants. Was he going to toss me out the door naked?

"Engaged," he grumbles as he pulls his shirt over his head. From the sounds of it, he wasn't looking for a response from me.

"Fucking asshole thinks she's his," he snarls quietly.

His dark eyes lock on mine, and I can see that he's none too pleased with my state of undress or lack thereof.

"Clothes, now," he snaps.

My hands move a little faster now. Something about the words Gage was mumbling and grumbling about said he's about to prove the invisible owner wrong.

As my bra hit the floor, I lifted my head to look at him. But instead, I found the world spinning as he turned me roughly. He proceeds to shove my chest flush onto the bed. My ass was now sticking up in the air, and my feet were still on the floor.

"I'll fucking show everyone that you belong to me," he growls as he lines his thick cock up to my entrance. There was no other warning. No foreplay. Just a quick, harsh thrust and he forced his massive dick into my pussy. Forcing me to take every inch of him.

My mouth dropped open as a loud screamed moan is forced from me. There was a bit of pain mixed within the intense pleasure.

One of his hands gripped my hip, and the other weaved through my brown locks. He then pulled my head back, and I was lifted a few inches off the bed, causing me to bow slightly.

"This pussy is mine," he snarls as he pounded into me from behind. His hold forced me to take everything he wanted to give.

Screams of pleasure filled the room, mixing with the sound of flesh hitting flesh. Wet noises were coming from my pussy every time his cock pulled out and slammed back into me.

As a result, the bed hit the wall over and over, and my hips hit the mattress, forcing me to bounce forward.

"I fucking own this. You. Are. Mine!" He shouts as he pounded into me, impossibly harder.

His heavy cock thrusts in and out of me, hitting my womb on each return. The pleasure was just too much.

"I will fill you full of my cum until I fucking knock you up!" he roars. Those words sent me over the edge. My whole body stiffened and shook as he plowed past my spasming walls.

I felt his hot breath as he leaned over my back, using his weight to push his dick in as far as it would go.

"Fucking understand me, you are mine. This pussy is mine. No one is going to take you from me," Gage growls. "And sweetness, if I have to keep you barefoot and pregnant, I will."

His cock twitched, and then he was filling me over and over with his hot thick cum. His dirty, naughty words sent me into another smaller climax.

I waited for him to pull out, but he surprised me when he lifted my hips slightly, pulling me further onto his cock. He was making sure that I was at an angle, so his cum stayed deep inside me.

The man was crazy. He was trying to ensure his seed took root. For the first time, I was truly afraid of him. Zec was going to get me, and pregnant wasn't going to be a good thing.

Chapter 22

Ronnie

Present Day.

The last two weeks together have been amazing. The only thing making it hard were the secrets. They were easier to keep with Gage making runs. He was getting ready for something, but he wouldn't tell me about it.

I had a very good idea as to what, but I didn't want to think too hard on it. If I did, it could be the end of the line for me.

After the pounding that he just gave me. I was limp and ready for a nap. Learning some of my secrets this morning sent him into a caveman frenzy.

The other secrets, well technically, there was only one. I was going to turn myself over to Zec before anyone died for me.

"What's on your bucket list?" The question came from left field, and it had me looking at him in complete confusion.

"Huh?"

"What are the things that you want to do more than anything?" he asks with a shrug.

That was a good question. I never put together a bucket list besides escaping the hell that awaited me. What did I want to do? It's not like I had much time left in this world.

"Is it that long?"

I smile and shake my head. I couldn't tell him the truth, and I couldn't confess that I wouldn't be long for this world.

"I want to ride on the back of your bike."

I scramble to think of other simple things. Ones that I could do quickly.

"That's it?"

"No, give me a moment!"

"I want to dance under the stars. I want to have sex in the rain. I want to eat a s'more, swim in the ocean, I want…" I hesitate. The last one was a doozy.

"What? You want what?" He prods.

"I want to get married," I shrug like its no big deal. Truthfully, when I ran, I never wanted to get married. But I want to die with a different last name just to know that I was truly free. That I did everything most women do and some crazy things too. I want to know what it feels like to be loved. Truly loved.

"Married?"

"Yes," I say firmly. It was true, I did. And I wanted it to be just Gage and only Gage.

He was entirely too quiet. I feared that I pushed too hard.

"Get dressed," he tells me while giving me a quick hard smack on the ass.

"Ouch, asshole," I growl.

He was already getting dressed when I sat up. My brows scrunch together. What the fuck was he going to do?

"Something nice," he tells me with a wink.

With that, he was gone. I was left to stare at the closed door, wondering what the fuck just happened.

Chapter 23

Ronnie

Present Day.

Riding on the back of his bike was like flying. The air whipped around us and tugged at my lose locks of hair. My arms wrap around him, and his back started heating my front.

I had no fucking idea where we were going or why we were following Crow and Maria. A small part of me feared it was to hand me over, but I didn't want to ruin this beautiful moment by asking.

After Gage left, he went into the meeting Crow demanded earlier. Maria appeared at the bedroom door with a beautiful dress. The white top flowed into a light teal.

She had to push and prod until I finally put the thing on, and it came to my knees. She then handed me a pair of white and teal sneakers, and I looked at her in confusion.

She gave me one look, and I also put them on. After everything, I told her this morning, her willingness to do something nice for me made it hard to open my mouth.

When we stopped, I looked around utterly lost. Then I saw the courthouse looming in front of us. No, this couldn't be happening.

"Come on, sweetness,' Gage's deep voice had my heart fluttering. Taking his hand, I slowly climbed from the back of his bike.

"If this is what I think it is, you're insane," I tell him with a laugh.

"Then, I'm insane."

Turning, I looked at him again. He was serious. My heart fluttered.

"Really?" I ask him.

"You're already mine, baby. This is just a formality."

Maria comes skipping over and grabs my hand pulling me to the courthouse. She was laughing as we both started running.

I was getting married. Turning my head, I looked back at Gage as he followed behind us. For a moment, I feared he was going to change his mind and run.

As the doors swung open, we walked into the lobby, and my eyes misted. Maria grabs the white roses from the lady behind the counter and pulls me into a little room.

Gage appeared next to me. We shared our vows, exchanged rings, and then his lips were on mine.

"Forever and always, I do," I whispered to him as his lips claim mine again.

"I love you," he whispers into my ear as he pulls me in close to his body.

"I love you, too."

He lets Maria push him aside so she could pull me into a hug. I wrapped my arms around her and sighed. I thought I lost this.

"Come on, baby. We have something to do." Gage grabs my arm and pulls me out of the courthouse and down the steps.

"Where are they going?" I ask as I point to Crow and Maria.

"To get the party ready," Gage replied with a casual shrug.

Climbing back onto his bike, I press a kiss to the back of his neck. I wrap my arms around his waist and hold him close. Those amazing calloused fingers wrap around my hands and squeeze.

"Hold on tight, baby," he shouts as he takes off with a squeal of the tires.

My eyes slam shut as we drive down the windy roads at a downright terrifying speed.

I smelled it before I opened my eyes. The salty air had my lungs expanding, and my chest tightening.

"The ocean," I whisper into his ear.

I look at the beautiful water as the sun beams down on it, making it sparkle.

"I don't have a swimsuit," I tell him.

"Baby, you can go naked, and I would die a happy fucking man," he laughs as I swat at him.

"Bra and panties," he tries again.

Looking around, I realized there wasn't anyone here.

"I wouldn't take you someplace that had a bunch of people. I don't want anyone looking at what's mine," he growled as he pulled me into his hard chest.

His lips met mine in a deep kiss. My toes curled in my shoes and my pussy clenched on air. Squeezing my knees together, I try to alleviate the ache to no avail.

"Dress off, baby."

The sound of his voice had me obeying. Something tells me if it's not off, it'll get wet. I then pulled my shoes and dress off and draped them over the seat of his bike.

"Alright…" everything I was going to say got lost on a scream as I'm thrown over his shoulder. As soon as I'm up there, he's running.

"Going to be cold," he shouts as he runs into the waves, taking me with him. Just as I open my mouth to yell at him, I'm flying through the air and being swallowed by the cold salty water.

Every muscle froze for a moment. It felt like I was swimming in melting ice. Breaching the surface, I quickly stood and started running. Not further into the water, but out of it.

My lips, I'm sure, was a shade of blue that could be considered lipstick. My whole body was shaking and covered in goosebumps.

Laughter erupts from me as I ran as fast as my stiff body could go. The water in Maine was freezing.

"Where you going?" Gage asks, his voice straining with laughter.

"Away from here!" I scream as more laughs fall from my frozen lips.

"Thought you wanted to swim in the ocean?" He laughs harder, making the words almost hard to hear.

Looking over my shoulder, I stick up my middle finger. "Did that, thanks!"

My eyes widen as he starts moving in my direction with determination written all over his handsome face. Oh god, I wasn't going back in there. Not fucking happening.

To my utter relief, he didn't plunge me back into the depths of where, I'm sure, jack frost takes a bath. Instead, he lays me down on the sandy beach and fucks the life out of me.

Having sex on the beach wasn't on my list, but it sure the hell made its way there quickly.

Chapter 24

Ronnie

Two Days Later.

I should feel something right now, but everything was drained from me. I looked around the secluded barn with new eyes. What I thought was a sweet moment turned into nothing but the club's chip to freedom.

Zec's cold, calculating eyes landed on me. The darkness swirled along with anger. They were dark, glittering coals of menace, and I could see the promise in them.

I didn't bother looking at Gage. It was over. Including the free air and beautiful moments. All the things that I thought I could have flashed in my mind.

Like a kaleidoscope of bright colors flashing too fast to catch a glimpse of one single moment.

I resisted the urge to palm my stomach. I found out yesterday morning that I was pregnant. I was going to tell Gage last night, but instead, he took me dancing under the stars.

My fairy tale was over, and this was it. I was no longer the woman that I wanted to be. I was who everyone else wanted me to be. They acted like I was just going to go along with it. Fuck that! I was going to be who my child needed me to be.

"Rosaline," Zec's cool voice had goosebumps rise all over my body.

"Zec," I smiled.

"Come here, now," the coldness in his voice lashed at me like a whip covered in ice.

Swallowing the fear that wanted to strangle me, I let my feet pull me closer to the man who's going to destroy me.

I wanted to laugh. Zec missed his chance, and Gage successfully took what he wanted so badly. But, Gage destroyed me, leaving this hollowness behind. This empty pit of nothingness.

Pain radiated over my face, and my eyes watered. A small cry left my lips, and I hated myself for the weakness. Zec's hand raised again as if to go for another blow. Blood filled my mouth from the cut on my split lip, I could still feel the pain, but I wasn't going to show it.

I turned and spat my blood-filled saliva onto the floor. Looking back at Zec, I grinned a huge smile which was covered in blood.

If I was going out of this world, I was going out fighting. Raising my hand, I held my palm out, bending my fingers, giving Zec the come get me motion as I slowly backed away.

"You want me, come get me, motherfucker," I scream as I lunge backward.

I didn't look around for a friendly face. I didn't look for help, I knew there was none.

My hair flew around my face as an arm wrapped around my waist, knocking the air from my lungs. Zec pulled me back into a hard, firm unforgiving body. Before the air had returned to my lungs, I was being handed off.

"Take her to the house," Zec demands coldly.

The person he handed me to latched onto my arm and pulled me hard. His grip was harsh, and his blunt nails pierced my flesh. But I refused to show the pain it caused. Swallowing, I kept my head forward.

"Are we done here? I have shit to do," Gage asks just as I was pulled out into the blinding light of the sun.

His tone was devoid of any emotion as if he was handing over a cigarette or beer. Like I was an object and nothing more. There was no affection, no regret.

This was really happening. Gage was handing me over to Zec. I wanted to cry, scream, and beg him to save me. To save us.

Instead, my head tilted back, and the sun caressed my face. This may be the last time that I could feel or see the sunshine.

The hand on my arm tugged me harder, and my heels dug into the ground. The man continued to pull me closer to the tinted windows of the dark sedan.

Once I was in that car, it was over. My hand touched my stomach, and I sent a silent prayer. I begged for my child. Don't let it suffer for my mistakes or my choices.

The phone Maria had given me was stuffed in my pocket. I knew it was soon to be smashed on the side of some road. The watch Gage gave me this morning felt more of a shackle than a sign of love. I wanted to rip it from my wrist and shove it down his lying, heartless throat.

Please give me the chance to kick him in the balls. I need only two things. One, to save my child and two, let me kick Gage's balls into his throat. I would gladly give my life for those two things. The ring on my finger never felt tighter, never felt as cold, or as fake as it did at this moment.

Looking back, I should have seen this coming. The last few days Gage checked off all the items on my bucket list. Marrying me was something he did easily. It would be over in a few days. Fuck him. Fuck them all.

Chapter 25

Gage

Yesterday.

"The fuck I do! That's my wife your talking about!" I snarl at Crow. My old lady, my wife. Who the fuck does he think he is? My chest heaves as anger and fear fought a battle inside me.

"Listen to me. I don't like it anymore then you do, but we need to get the location dammit. We'll get Ronnie back," Crow shouts.

"Easy for you to say. You're not the one giving your wife over to a fucking psychopath!"

"He knows the location of Maria's sister, and we need to do this," he tells me coldly.

"Fuck her sister! The backstabbing bitch! Let them fucking kill her," I snarl.

He wanted to give my wife to the Albanian mob. To get the junkie who sold out his old lady and kid. What the fuck was wrong with him?

"There's more to it than that."

"The fuck there is. You just want to make Maria happy. Well, I'm pretty sure handing over the woman that saved her isn't going to make her happy."

Crow leans back heavily in his seat. His eyes were tortured and dark.

"Fucking listen to me. When Zec takes her, we'll track them, and then we'll kill the fucking assholes." Crow sighs.

"While Ronnie endures whatever the fuck he wants to her? Fuck you, Crow!"

I half expect some bullshit from Knox or Weston, but neither has pipped in on this.

"I'm going to kill her fucking sister, but if we don't play the fuck along, we won't get Ronnie free from this fucking asshole," Crow says darkly.

I couldn't hand her over. The thought of Zec touching her, hurting her was tearing me up inside.

"Don't make me do this," I beg him.

"She can't know," he tells me before leaving the room.

I thought it was done, but he looks at me and says something that has me flying out of my chair.

"Tomorrow, Gage. The meet is at the old barn on Wilton road."

Bloodlust. Something I've been dealing with since prison, but Ronnie calms me. She made me feel human again. Now, I need to hand her over without a fucking explanation.

None of my brothers would meet my eyes as I walked out of the room. Tonight, I would fulfill the last thing on her bucket list. Tomorrow, I would lose her. Possibly forever.

Chapter 26

Ronnie

Present Day.

The room, if you can call it that, was dark. How much time has passed? Where am I? I knew I wasn't home, the drive wasn't that long.

"There she is," Zec's dark, angry voice fills the once silent room.

"I fucking hate you," I scream at him.

Either way, he was going to kill me and not in a quick 'how do you do' way. It was going to be painful, and I knew he was going to force me to accept him.

I would endure this with all the grace that I could muster. Freedom was always an option if I am still breathing. When it comes to that, just check out, and be somewhere else. Pretend you're anywhere but here.

Strong words to myself, and I want to laugh. It wouldn't just be Zec, it will be his brother and any of his men that want a piece. I was ruined, and no longer suitable to be a wife.

"Now, I need to make sure everyone sees what happens when you fucking run. And for that, we need to go home," Zec sounds almost gleeful.

My shoulders sag. I have a little more time before he destroys what little Gage had.

"But that doesn't mean I can't play a little now," Zec laughs as something cracks through the air.

"Get her shirt off," he commands.

Feet pound into the room as I scramble backward in the dark while looking for a place to hide. The only light was from the opening where Zec now stands.

Harsh hands grab me as something cold touches the skin at the back of my neck. I freeze instantly. They could easily just force it down and sever my spine from my neck.

A quick death, my mind whispers. Freedom, close at hand. For a moment, I think about trying to force it, but I can't. The baby deserves to live, and I was going to fight to make sure that happened.

"Tie her to the pole," Besin demands.

The sound of fabric rendering filled the room. More hands latch onto me. One was tying my wrists together while another lifted me off the ground and carried me into the middle of the room. Or at least, I think it's the middle.

Fear like I've never felt before strangles me. Something cold touches my hands as I get pushed into the metal pole that Besin was referring too.

Another loud crack splits the air, but this time, I felt it, and my skin burns. Then another crack, this time I felt my back split under the force of the hard leather whip.

Another lash and more blood dripped down my back as my screams of pain mix with my tears.

"I'm going to play with you, Rosaline. First, with this whip, then with a knife, and finally with my cock," he laughs coldly.

The blood began to drip from the gashes and drain by my feet. After Zec was done, I was going to be a broken shell, and the baby would definitely be no more.

I cried. Not for my fate, not to be saved, but for the loss, I could feel coming. Was freedom, the small taste that I had, worth this?

Then there was more searing pain, more blood, more screams, and more tears. No one was coming for me. That was something I wished for. I had to hold onto hope, but I had no hope left.

"Leave us," Zec commands after what feels like hours. The sound of shuffling feet mix with my quiet, stuttering breaths.

"I need to have you now. I'll cut little pieces off after I fuck you," Zec tells me.

The room was so quiet, I could hear him undoing his belt. The button on his pants releases and the zipper slowly lowers.

I wait for him to tear at my clothes. But I hear feet moving, and then something hitting the floor hard. Still, I keep them closed. Something like hope tries to blossom, and I know this is a part of the game.

Whatever hit the floor was being dragged closer to me. My breath hitched, and then I screamed. I tried to pull away and kick with my legs.

"Shhh, baby. I've got you," Gage's deep voice filled the room. It was so full of pain, I just knew I dreamt it up.

"I'll kill you. Don't touch me," I scream, as I pull as hard as I can on my bound hands. I was trying to pull away from this mean, cruel trick.

"Baby, please," his voice was filled with tears. "What did he do to you?"

My heart was turning into dust. It couldn't take any more of this pain.

"Just do it," I whisper as I sag.

There was no escape, at least not on the outside. Right now, I was drifting. Living in the moment before he handed me over to Zec.

The stars loomed above us like glittering stones. The music drifted as he wrapped me up in his arms and danced slowly with me.

The air was cooler than it was earlier today, but I felt nothing but warmth as his body pressed closer to mine. His lips pressed against my forehead.

I was where I wanted to be, even if it was a dream. No one could hurt or touch me here.

In my dream, I was with him, and we were building a family. Life was perfect, and I was finally free.

Chapter 27

Gage

Present Day.

Her screams ripped through me like poison arrows. I dragged a dying Zec over towards her. Slitting his throat was something I relished, even if I wanted nothing more then to rip him apart. One piece at a time.

We slowly entered the house very quietly. Too fucking slow, in my opinion. It took me ten minutes to find her. When I finally did, what I saw will haunt me for the rest of my life.

That motherfucker was taking off his pants. So, I slipped up behind him and covered his mouth. I then cut his dick off and slit his throat.

Her screams filled the room as she struggled to get away from me. Her back was covered in red. What terrified me the most was when she went limp. Telling me to just do it and then she checked out.

Reaching over, I untied her hands and gently pulled her into my lap. My knees ached from where they hit the floor. The site of her brought me to my knees.

A shadow filled the door, but my eyes stayed on Ronnie. My shaking hand brushed the hair from her face. She had her eyes closed, and she wasn't moving.

Leaning down, I listened as she took a breath and released it. For a fucking moment, I thought she was dead. That I had lost her.

"Is she....?" Crow's voice filled the room.

"Fuck you," I snarl. I pulled Ronnie closer to me and rocked her gently.

"Shh, I've got you. I love you, baby." I tell her over and over.

"We need to go. Zec's brother got away, the fucking coward," Crow growls.

I don't look at him or any of my brothers. I just lifted Ronnie and cradled her to my chest. I was trying to keep my hands away from her back.

No one said a word as we made our way out of that hell hole. Weston was currently setting it all on fire. No one tried to stop me as I laid her down in the backseat of the SUV and climbed in with her. I rested her head on my lap and gently caressed her tangled blood covered brown locks of hair.

Her back was torn up, bad. Zec whipped her, and I wished I could kill him all over again. Slowly.

Chapter 28

Ronnie

One Week Later.

"Come back to me, baby. Please, I need you," Gage's voice filled my ears.

I didn't want to leave wherever I was. It was beautiful, and our life was perfect. It was filled with love and laughter.

"I love you," he whispered as he kissed my forehead.

My heart fluttered at the feeling. I love you, too. I wanted to tell Gage, but I wasn't there. I was here. In a world of beauty and peace.

"Is she going to ever come out of this?" I heard him ask someone.

"There's no real way to know. It could happen now or never." A bright light hit my eyes. "Wherever her mind took her, she feels safe and doesn't want to come back."

A calloused hand shifted through my hair, and a kiss was pressed into my shoulder.

"I need you. Do you hear me? I can't do this without you," Gage tells me.

"If not for me, please come back for our baby," he commands.

Of course, he demands. Baby. Baby. Baby. The word swirls in my head like a little tornado. My hands cup my stomach, there was a baby in there that needs me.

"Ronnie?" Gage whispers, leaning in close so he can look into my eyes. His hand cups my cheek, rubbing it gently.

"Come back to me," he whispers. Tears fill my eyes. I blink them away quickly as more take their place.

I could tell that I was laying on my side. It was the way the bed felt under my hip that caused a frown to pull between my brows. I was on my side.

Then it hit me. Zec, the whip, and his promises. I screamed. My throat was raw and dry as pain and sorrow filled me. No, I want to go back.

"There she is," that annoying voice made me want to commit a crime.

"Shh, I've got you, baby," I heard and recognized the voice.

Don't touch me! Get away from me!" I'm screamed. I didn't give a shit if my throat felt like it was on fire.

"I had to give you to him. I fucking hated it, baby. I got to you as fast as I could." He tried to grab my face with both hands. Attempting to cup my cheeks.

"NO!" I scream. "You gave me to him. I thought you loved me," I sobbed painfully.

"Fuck, baby. I do love you. I fucking love you more than life itself," his voice was hoarse with unshed tears. I could see them shimmering in his eyes.

"Why? Why did you do this to me?"

"We had to. It was the only way we could kill him. I didn't want to give you over, sweetness. You have to believe me," he begs.

I was being torn apart. I wanted to believe Gage, and I wanted to just forget. Tears streamed down my face in heated trails.

"He wanted to take my head for demanding this," Crow announces.

My eyes dart to him. He was standing in the doorway looking at me. I could see he was telling the truth and that he was sorry.

Fuck him. Crow didn't have to go through what I did.

"Thought I needed to experience what Maria did? Is that why you did this to me?" I accused.

Regret filled his eyes. His head shook back and forth.

"Feel better about it now? Should I thank you? Well, thank you for saving my life. Is that what you came in here for?" I lash out harshly.

"I'm sorry, Ronnie. You were never supposed to get hurt."

Closing my eyes, I sighed. In the end, he freed me. As much as I wanted to hate him, they gave me what I always dreamed of. True freedom.

"I understand," I tell him quietly.

As he turned to leave, I tell him, "I forgive you."

The tension in his body released. His eyes met mine, and I could see the sorrow and pain that he was feeling. Then he was gone.

"I love you, Ronnie," Gage said, pulling my attention back to him.

"Do you?" I sounded like a vicious viper.

"I fucking hate that you even need to ask me that," he says before lowering his head.

"I love you, too," I whisper pressing a kiss to the top of his head.

"I wanted to tell you. I wanted to fucking kill Crow for making me do this," Gage sighed, his head was pressed into the mattress.

"Gage, I understand." And I did. His president gave him an order. He had no choice but to follow it. I grew up in the mob life, and you followed orders. Period.

"I love you, baby. So fucking much," he tells me as he raised his head and pressed a kiss to my lips.

There was one thing I needed to know, but I was terrified of the answer. As if Gage could read my mind, he shook his head no.

"I killed him before he could."

That's all I needed. I should be angry, resentful, and full of the need for vengeance. Gage saved me and gave me a real life. A future.

"You pull this shit again, and I'll castrate you," I tell him coldly.

Epilogue

Nine Months Later.

Our son Killian cooed from his bassinet as I heated up his bottle. He may seem calm now, but in a few minutes, he will be screaming loud enough to bring the roof down on our heads.

The sound of someone knocking on the door had a frown forming on my face. Gage made his way to the door, and whoever was there wasn't talking loud enough to be heard this far into the house.

Turning back to the bottle, I shrug.

"I've got the bottle," Gage tells me before placing a kiss to my neck.

Something in me clenches. This couldn't be good. I know for a fact it's not Maria. She doesn't wait by the door, she barges in.

Pulling the door open, I gasp in shock. There's no fucking way it's her. This is some fucked up dream I'm going to hate waking up from.

"Rosaline?" Her sweet voice was full of concern.

"Savanna?" I ask, my voice filled with the shock I was sure was written all over my face.

"Can I come in?" She asks as she looks around the deserted area behind her.

"Of course."

"I'm sorry. I know I shouldn't be here, but you told me if I wanted the freedom, I should find you," Savanna says, her eyes begging me to help her.

"I've got you," I promise her.

Her shoulders drop as she lets out a deep sigh of relief.

"I did something bad. I didn't make a clean break Rosaline."

"Come on. Let's go into the kitchen."

Gage nods as he walks past us. A burp cloth over one shoulder and a baby bottle in his hand. I watch as he disappears into the living room before turning to Savanna.

"Tell me everything."

Learn about what happens with Savanna in Breaking Weston coming soon.

The End.

Begging Topher
Grimm Brothers MC Book 5

Prologue:

Two Years Ago.

It wasn't always like this. The grind of filth and fear. There as a time we were happy and safe. When mom and dad were still here, and not off with a new family or god knows where.

She loved us, and we were happy. I'm not sure the exact moment that changed, just one day she was gone.

The calls and visits became less and less. My sister would put on a brave face trying to lessen the blow of being unwanted and replaced.

Even then I kept the belief that sometimes bad things happen. It even occurred in those fairytale books, and I hoped everything would all work out in time.

My sister told me when I was fourteen that it was okay to believe in fairytales. She said we were all programmed to believe in them, it was a human flaw.

We believe that when a boy pushed you, called you names or stole your cookie that he just had a crush on you. Then as we got older, we believed that if he's spending less time with you or calling less that he's just playing hard to get. Or maybe he's keeping things fresh in the relationship.

My sister said that we lie to ourselves and to our friends. I just smiled and told her that there were cases where love prevailed. When the couple had that sweet happily ever after even though there were turmoil and mistakes along the way.

I wasn't willing to settle. I knew my soulmate was out there waiting for me. At no point would I say, 'oh, this is good enough. I could have a good life with this man.' No. I wanted it to be more like the flowers are duller, the air less fresh, and the sun less bright without that special someone.

Chapter 1
Brittany
Six Months Ago.

My sister Tori looked at me like I was an alien species that needed to be probed and maybe even dissected. She saved money for my birthday, and I had wanted only one thing.

A tattoo. And not just any tattoo. Nope, I wanted roses. I wanted them to be red like the ones in Beauty and the Beast. It's one of my favorite fairy tales.

Unlike the other stories, he wasn't perfect. He had the flaws, the emotions, and the rawness the other charmers didn't have. And Bell? She was different as well. She had a love of books and the ability to see under the surface. I felt a slight kinship to her.

I watched as my sister scanned the images. They were scattered on paper the size of a poster and enclosed in a protective poster frame.

Each one was filled with different tattooed images. Mine? Wasn't in there, it was different. I wanted it to have more than one rose, and I didn't want the stems. I only wanted the cluster of red bloomed roses.

This way there were more chances for me to find the one. And more time before the petals fell. I asked myself again, what did my prince charming look like? Would I know the moment our eyes met?

Why did I think Ronald was that man? I had a date with him tonight. Another long night of hearing about how sexy I was. Honestly, it was exhausting. The more time I spent with him, the more I realized he definitely wasn't the one.

The idea of breaking up on my birthday though, it made me cringe. My face twisted at the thought and Tori looked at me a little more closely.

"Does it hurt?" She asked.

"Not really," I tell her truthfully.

"Then why the sour face?" She asked with a frown.

"Ronald," I replied with a twist of my lips. It was a rueful smile. I wanted what he couldn't give me.

She shuddered. I knew she hated Ronald. That should have been a sign that this wasn't meant to be. Because honestly, my prince should be someone my sister could coo as family.

Why had I let our relationship get this far? Sometimes I questioned my need for this other person. Did I really need this faceless man to complete my life?

"Stand him up," she tells me with a shrug and a cruel tilt of her lips.

I thought about it. Did that make me a horrible person? The man outlining the roses on my skin spoke up, "Sounds like you're not interested, leave his ass hanging."

My sister laughed hard, and I felt myself smile. Not only because of the man's words but because my sister was laughing.

She didn't do that much. Not since dad left and she started working at that bar. My eyes closed. She hated it, and I hated her working there.

"You can spend the night with me. Dinner, take out, and maybe a movie? We can stop by the Redbox and rent one," she tells me with a smile.

We didn't spend enough time together. My sister worked so much, and something in me warmed. Why the hell would I go out with Ronald if I could have this night with my sister?

"Do I get to pick?" I asked her with a big Cheshire cat smile.

She hated romance movies, and I loved them. She believed that there was no such thing as love outside of the family. That it was a simulated emotion that after time people grew tired of faking.

"I guess," she tells me with a sigh.

Her smile took the sting out of her depressing sigh. I knew she loved me. She was the only person who did.

Her eyes took on a sadness. As if she could tell where my thoughts had gone. I knew she was thinking about what our life had become.

I blamed mom leaving us, but it was like a domino effect. She knocked over one, and they just kept falling. Dad started drinking and pretending that we didn't exist. It forced my sister to grow up fast and take care of me.

She put on so many brave faces so many times. I could see the hurt and sadness in her eyes as her friends went out and she was stuck home watching me.

It was like life was stolen from her. But not once did she complain about the burden that I was to her. She made sure that I felt loved and cherished.

"What about work?" I couldn't help but ask.

"I don't work tonight," she tells me quietly.

It was a lie, she worked every night. Would they punish her for not being there?

"Are you sure?" I pushed.

"Brit, don't worry about it, okay? That's my job," she gave me a loving smile.

But I was worried. I mustered up a smile then watched as my sister's shoulders slowly lost the tension. She laughed as I stuck my tongue out at her.

"I can't believe you're eighteen today," she tells me with a shake of her head.

"It's your birthday?" The tattoo artist asked.

He had paused as he dipped the tattoo gun into the black ink.

"Yeah," I shrugged.

He looked at me like he could read my soul. He turned and gave my sister the same deep penetrating stare.

"It's on the house, but don't tell anyone," he gave us a big smile.

My sister tenses. I could literally read it on her face. Payment was always required in some way.

"Don't look at me like that, Doll. I don't want any kind of payment," he empathized the last four words firmly.

She nodded looking down at her hands. My sister has dealt with some really nasty men. They all wanted something that she didn't want to give, and I was so fucking relieved they didn't just take it.

Chapter 2
Brittany
Six Months Ago.

Ronald was waiting by the door to our apartment. I stifled a scream that wanted to erupt from my throat. My heart then tried to beat out of my chest. Crap, I felt almost like I had a small heart attack.

"What are you doing here?" I asked him.

"Where have you been?" He growled while latching onto my arm painfully.

"Let me go," I tell him firmly.

"I fucking own you," he growled at me.

"Fuck you, Ronald, no one owns me," I tell him.

Anger and fear contorted inside of me like a small tornado. Heat rushed to my face as he pulled me closer to him.

"Why are you like this?" I asked him as I scanned the hallway hoping for someone to come to my rescue.

"Where the fuck have you been?" he shouts, leaning in so close that I could feel his heated breath against my lips. I give a small involuntary shudder. Oh god, don't get any closer.

"Out and you need to go before Tori gets here," I tell him firmly.

"Fuck your sister," Ronald snapped.

"Thanks, but no thanks," my sister's voice came from somewhere behind him.

"Stay the fuck out of this," he growled at Tori.

"Let her go and get the fuck out of here before I add a new hole to that body of yours," she tells him sweetly.

My eyes closed as a laugh tried to bubble out of me. Kind of like a bottle of dish soap shaken too hard. Slowly, I leaned to look over his shoulder.

My sister Tori stood there with her feet shoulder length apart. Her arms were out in front of her and a gun held perfectly in both hands. She looked like a badass from Charlie's Angels.

Ronald gripped my wrist tighter as he turned his head to look at my sister. He tensed as he took her in. I wondered what he thought as he looked down the barrel.

"Let her go now, Ronald. Then walk the fuck away," she snarled at him.

My shoulders lowered. I hadn't realized they were almost touching my ears. The muscles in my body loosened as the fear started to dissipate. I knew my sister would pull that trigger and would do it with the smile she currently had plastered to her face.

One finger after another slowly left my skin. When Ronald finally released me completely, he held up his hands with his palms out as he turned to look at my sister completely.

"Start walking," she snarled at him.

My eyes closed as I heard his retreating steps. Then I heard them hitting the stairs at an increasing speed.

"You okay?" Tori whispered as she pulled me into her body.

"I am now," I tell her with a shaky smile.

"Where have you been?" she asked me.

"I was out watching a late-night movie," I tell her.

She nodded. After the tattoo, she went and got me a gift certificate to the movie theater. A hundred dollars paid for a few movies and some snacks.

"Let's get inside, I need a shower," she tells me, changing the subject almost as if she knew I didn't want to talk about Ronald now.

Chapter 3
Topher
Six Months Ago.

Oh, Jerry, you stupid fucker. His sniffles did nothing but irritate me.

"Are you fucking done yet?" I snap at him.

I mean, I want to get something to eat and drink. Some whiskey, maybe a steak, and a baked potato. Hell, make it a loaded baked potato.

"I'm sorry. I'll do better," Jerry begged again.

Sighing, I crouched down with my wrist resting on my bent knee. My gun was hanging in my clutched hand.

"We went over this Jerry. There is no 'I'll do better,'" I tell him with an over exaggerated sigh.

"Please, one more chance," he pleaded his eyes, looking up into mine almost like he was hoping to pull at my heartstrings. Was he stupid? My heart was black and as hard as coal.

"Dig faster Jerry, or I'll start shooting those knees. They are looking particularly good right now," I tell him with a smirk.

Rusty, one of our prospects, laughed and I turned to look at him. Rusty has been with us for about a year now. It was about time we voted him in. I'll have to say something to Zane.

"Don't laugh too much you're the one filling the hole," I tell him.

"Fucker," he grumbled.

I laughed, and this time Jerry sobbed louder. God be a man for once Jerry and shut that shit down.

"Cruel as fuck man, making him dig his own grave," Rusty says.

"You want to dig it?" I asked him casually.

"Fuck, no," he laughs.

"Yeah, that's what I thought. So, shut the fuck up," I tell Rusty, my eyes go back to Jerry. Fuck, could he go any slower?

"Jerry, you're going to die. Dragging it out does not help you in any way," I tell him.

Rusty kicked a rock, and I watched as it bounced off Jerry's forehead. He cried out pausing in his digging to rub his head.

I glared at Rusty. "Listen, fucker. As much as that was comical, I'm hungry," my voice was harsh like I had too many smokes.

"Sorry, boss," he said sheepishly.

"It was funny as fuck though," I lightened my tone.

Rusty smiled and turned his attention back to Jerry who was currently wiping his snot on his dirty button up shirt.

"Come on Jerry, move this shit along," I prompted.

His bloodshot eyes looked up at me. They were watery and filled with terror. Why did he have to make this shit so difficult?

"I'm sorry," he tried again.

"There's no changing this. There will be no last-minute phone call like in the damn movies, Jerry. So, get this shit over with," I tell him aspirated.

He looks over towards Rusty like he was going to swoop in and save the day. Shaking my head, I raised my gun and fired it. The bullet hit the dirt just a foot from his leg.

His girlish scream had Rusty laughing. Jerry was our accountant. The keyword here is 'was' or it will be as soon as I put a nice new hole in the center of his forehead.

He thought he could move some money into an off-shore account that didn't belong to the club. Seems Jerry here was planning on retiring early.

I was going over the books when I noticed these charges and they were consistent. Always for the same damn thing and for the same amount. Kind of like a monthly bill.

So, I started backtracking it all. It went back for almost a year. Fucking Jerry had been ripping us off for a long time. We would have noticed this shit sooner if Sal wasn't such a fucking control freak.

When Reyes and Gunner killed Sal, Zane became president. Then I became vice president. First thing Zane had me do was look over the damn books.

Boring as fuck. At least it was until I realized shit was going to get interesting soon. Jerry was looking at me oddly as I started grabbing book after book. Sweat had begun to pop up on his forehead.

It didn't take long for him to cry and agree to send all the money back to our accounts. My knife regretted not getting to play with him a little more.

Taking a deep drag off my cigarette, I looked at the hole Jerry had dug himself. Shit, he did a good job. It was nice and deep, at least three feet over his five-foot-nine stature.

Flicking my smoke at his face, I watched as it hit its mark and Jerry flinched.

"Shovel," I demanded, holding out my hand.

His eyes watered even more as he lifted the handle in my direction. I made no move to lean forward. I made him stand on his toes to get the handle pressed into my palm.

Rusty was looking particularly eager to get this over with. Yeah, me and you both. I looked at my gun then I look towards Rusty.

"Want the honors?" I asked him.

I had been ready to just kill Jerry and leave, but Rusty had to fill the hole. So maybe, just maybe, he deserved the reward of putting down our stray dog.

"Fuck, yeah," he said with excitement and something like pleasure reflecting through his eyes.

"Goodbye, Jerry," I tell him as I straddled my bike. The unmistakable sound of a gunshot was muffled due to the sound of my roaring motor.

Prologue:
One Year Ago.

I didn't see the man until I was just upon him. I knocked into him as he was leaning against the brick building that I lived in.

"I'm so sorry," I tell him while I ran my fingers through my long brown, and now frizzy stressed out hair.

Everything was going well until I found Gary fucking Jess in his apartment fifteen minutes ago. I thought I would surprise him with a nice dinner. I should have fled the moment I heard the moaning and groaning.

I was an idiot, I chastised myself. I thought maybe he was hurt.

"Yeah, hurting all over her, maybe she was his band-aid? My mind whispered, or better yet, I bet he just tripped and fell. Oh, and his dick just happened to go in her vagina."

"I didn't mean... I'm sorry. I should have been looking where I was going," I tell him quietly.

My cold bottle of wine was an innocent bystander, just like this poor guy with his short brown hair and deep blue eyes. My bottle of wine fell and shattered all over the ground, and the red liquid seeped and flowed all over the black pavement. Blue pieces of glass littered the ground, like my heart.

I had been holding the bottle when I caught them together. I thought Jess was my friend, I was so wrong.

"Fuck," the man growled before turning fully to me. I was looking at the wine on the ground but looked up suddenly when I heard him growl. The deepest blue eyes were staring at me, and it was a little disconcerting. He was the most handsome man I've ever seen.

He took in my red-rimmed eyes and disheveled appearance. His eyes were seeing more then what was on the surface. This man was seeing deep inside of me.

"You okay?" He asked me gently, in a voice deep and rich.

"Sure, all is right with the world," I said with a hysterical laugh.

"I'm really sorry," I tell him quietly as I bent over to pick up the broken pieces of the bottle. Something I couldn't do for my heart.

"I'll get this, you go take a hot bath or something," the man tells me. His voice was filled with sinful promise.

"No, I stumbled into you, and this is my mess," I tell him firmly.

"Really, go," he tells me in a way that left no room for argument.

I looked up at him from my crouched position. I slowly raised my hand and put it in his stretched-out hand. As he helped me to my feet, I gave him a small smile as well as the pieces that I was able to collect. We put them in the plastic bag that was in my other hand.

"Thank you," I gave him my best fake smile and walked past him.

He didn't say a word as I disappeared inside. I felt like crap for more than one reason. Gary, Jess and now the hottest man to grace this earth has seen me at my worse.

Loving Dean
Mafia Generations Book 3

Chapter 1

CHARLOTTE

One Year Ago.

"Come on, I need my coffee," Someone grumbled behind me.

"I'm sorry," I tell them quickly as I rushed to fill the coffee pot again. I had already fumbled by pouring the coffee ground in without the filter.

"Lo," Mia says quietly. "It's okay," she tells me gently.

It wasn't okay. Nothing was okay, but I didn't have it in me to tell Mia that. Then another customer sighed loudly frustrated that I was taking too long.

Well, if you walked in on your best friend... *Ex-best friend,* my mind reminded me. Sorry, my ex-best friend fucking your boyfriend, you would also be all out of sorts.

Flashes of the night before intruded my thoughts. In one hand, I held a plastic bag and the other I held a bottle of wine. Moans and grunts were coming from Gary's room.

Concern filled me as I walked in that direction. Did Gary fall and hurt himself? He was in good shape, but anyone can get hurt.

The closer I got, the louder the sounds got. My eyes filled with unshed tears as I heard more than one voice. I pushed on the partially open door and stepped into the room.

Gary was on the bed kneeling behind a woman with long blond hair. She was on her hands and knees, and they were both naked.

The tears that had been lingering started to spill over as the scene played out before me. Gary was really going at it. Is this what people looked like having sex?

Relief flooded me since I haven't had sex with him yet. I haven't had sex with anyone, wanting to wait until I was married. I watched as if this was a bad horror movie. Then Gary turned his head my way, and his brown eyes widened.

They were shit brown, and I just now noticed that small detail. I never thought of Gary's eyes being that color while we dated. Jess also turned her head to look at me.

Her green eyes grew bigger as she tried to move out from under Gary. Although, he had his hands clamped on her hips and held her in place.

I must have made some sort of distressed sound. His hips kept moving even though he looked ready to be sick. Actually, I was ready to be sick, oh god, how many have there been?

Gary and I have been dating a year and two months. Jess and I have been friends for three years. How often has this happened? My chest constricted, and I pulled the bottle of wine to my chest as if it could comfort me. Like an old beloved teddy bear.

"Lo," Mia said gently, pulling me from my thoughts.

I've known Mia since high school. We've been friends since the third day of high school. I turned and looked at her.

"Why don't you take a fifteen-minute break. I've got this," Mia tells me quietly.

Looking over my shoulder, I took in the long line of frustrated patrons and gave her a nod.

Without a word, I walked quickly into the back room. I found a box, and sat down letting the world settle around me.

Chapter 2

DEAN

One Year Ago.

I've been watching Willow when Gary's girlfriend all but threw her bottle of wine at me. Judging by the look in her eyes, I knew she finally caught him in the act.

I felt something for her, and that didn't happen very often in my line of work. You learned to cut off any emotional ties that didn't benefit you or your job. There was family and *family*.

Her eyes were full of unshed tears as she pulled at her hair with her now free hand. I wasn't sure she even knew she was doing it.

She squatted down and started to carefully pick up the broken pieces of glass. I heard her apologize and she made some sort of reply.

I was surprised when I offered to clean up the mess, considering I was the victim and nowhere near a nice guy. Fuck, people who knew me called me an asshole.

"Really, go," I tell her firmly.

Why the fuck did this seem important?

"Thank you," she tells me, her voice was barely a whisper.

I didn't say a word as she disappeared into the building. I had been leaning up against Willow's house since it was next door. From what I could tell, Willow was her only real neighbor.

As soon as Cole got his ass back here, I was heading into Gary's as the fucker's card had just been punched. Tonight, Gary was going to die.

Chapter 3

CHARLOTTE

Eleven Months Ago.

He was back, well not really. The man that I bumped into was standing in line waiting for coffee. I felt little butterflies erupt in my stomach. My hands instinctively tried to fix my hair, but I kept them on the task of filling another coffee cup.

It was strange, we just kept meeting, and it was almost stalker like. But who was the stalker me or wine guy? A small laugh escaped at the thought. It was the first real carefree moment I've felt in quite some time.

My eyes found his profile again, and I tried not to linger, afraid I'd get caught. I took in his sun-kissed skin, dark brown hair, and the way his lips curved sensually.

Swallowing, I looked down at my hands fighting the need to clench them. I wanted to run my fingers through wine guys hair as I scream his name.

Oh god, what was wrong with me? I didn't even know his name let alone, wait… I can't go there. I bet he was an asshole. He was too good looking to be anything but. I knew assholes, and this man oozed it.

Sighing I tried to focus on the task at hand. But I couldn't bring myself to pretend the guy wasn't there. That this sinfully handsome man wasn't standing in the lobby even if he was most likely a dick.

My hands trembled as I thought of him between my thighs licking and biting. Oh god, I couldn't stop. I couldn't shut it off.

My eyes cast to the clock only ten more minutes of this before I could pull off my apron and rush out of the building like it was on fire.

I knew something that was on fire, and it wasn't something I could run from. Damn, wine guy licked his lips while looking at me, my body just went into overdrive. I wanted this man with an unparallel need. It was almost unhealthy.

"Char?" Mia whispered.

I turned to look at her, but she was focused on my hands. My eyes returned to them and saw that they were trembling.

"You can go home," she tells me gently.

I was sure she thought this was due to exhaustion or that my father had me on edge. This was actually my second job.

Dad's medical expenses were drowning us in debt. I took this job, so we didn't starve. We shared my apartment up until recently when he was once again admitted to the hospital.

I should feel relief or maybe do a dance that he was in there again. He was suffering like I have all these years.

My mother passed away when I was seven, and my father turned into a drunk. His breath was always putrid with the stench of alcohol. I hated when he twisted his fist in my shirt since I could smell his breath in my face.

His anger contorted his features and tears would fill my eyes as he shook me like a rag doll. I never knew what was going to set him off. Yet here I was, all those torturous years later caring for the man.

When I was sixteen, I wanted to go on a date, and it would be my first real one. The dance was coming up, and I so badly wanted to go. I even went as far as saving every penny from all the bottle deposits to save for this oversized dress from goodwill. I had hand stitched the seam to make it smaller. It still didn't fit, but it covered me.

When my dad saw me, he latched onto me. His hand crushed my upper arm as he leaned in. The smell of alcohol reeked from him, and his eyes looked crazed as he called me a whore. He actually slapped me across the face. The night of the dance he locked me in my room and refused to answer the front door for Tom, my date.

So many memories had me question why I was killing myself now to help a man who nothing did but bring me down and make me feel like nothing.

My dad was the reason why I kept going after all the Gary's of the world. The cheating no good bastard! And for some stupid reason, I continued to do it.

Slipping the apron over my head, I nodded to Mia. I tried to say thank you, but my throat closed and refused to open. I couldn't get any words out.

The line was shorter as I returned from the back. Clocking out only took a few minutes but Mia had already cleared half the lobby.

My eyes scanned the patrons. Wine guy was gone, and my heart sank.

It's for the best he's probably another Gary, I tell myself. If only I could believe it.

Chapter 4

DEAN

Ten Months Ago.

This was just another job, another night but they were starting to blend together. Blood and gore, their screams and cries were all becoming the same in my mind.

I was watching another target dance through the living room. This woman's beauty was astounding, but that was only skin deep. This bitch was horribly sick, her insides probably were black and reeking.

She would die tonight for her nasty behavior. She killed the soon-to-be wife of one of the dons that my father knew. She was jealous that the other woman would be in his arms. Not because she loved him, but for the power, she was losing in the match.

Taking a deep breath, I let it loose just as something collided with me from behind. A soft feminine oomph rented the air and had me twist to collect the girl before she hit the concrete sidewalk.

Her eyes were a beautiful shade of brown that sparkled as the light danced over them.

"Oh god, I'm so...," she swallows deeply "I'm so sorry," she sighed.

I watched in fascination as my previous target's ex-girlfriend tugged on her white V-neck. She adjusted the strap that crossed over her chest with her black leather purse.

This isn't the first time I've seen her over the last two months. I've seen her at the coffee shop where she worked and also at the grocery store.

The last time she didn't notice me, but I noticed her. She was hard not to notice with her long brown hair and sparkling brown eyes. Her short yet perfect body filled her jeans to perfection.

My arms were still holding her close, and her scent filled my every breath. She smelled like cherries, sweet, delicious cherries.

"You okay darin'?" My voice was low, and I watched in satisfaction as a little shudder moved over her.

She was feeling it too, and that thought brought a smile to my face.

"I keep doing this, I'm really sorry," she whispered while lowering her head.

"Don't worry about it darlin'," I tell her gently.

My eyes scanned her body taking in the tight as fuck blue jeans that looked painted on and the tight white V-neck t-shirt she wore. I could see the hint of pink from her bra through the thin material. I couldn't help but wonder if it was lacey or it if was more modest.

"If this keeps happening, I might die from embarrassment. I'm not normally this clumsy," she tells me with a weak smile.

"Really? I wouldn't have guessed," I tease her.

Her cheeks turned a pretty shade of pink only a little darker than the pink bra she wore.

"I need to go," she whispered and shook her head.

Slowly, my arms lower until they were against my sides. I felt as though I was losing something as she gave me a brief smile and dashed off like the hounds of hell were nipping at her heels.

You can run darlin', but eventually, I'll catch up to you. One of these little visits is going to go in my favor.

Made in United States
North Haven, CT
09 April 2025